DIARY OF A THUG

JAMES G. TANNER, JR.

Diary of a Thug by James G. Tanner, Jr.

This is a work of fiction. The author has invented the characters. Any resemblance to actual persons, living or dead, is purely coincidental.

ISBN: 978-0-9797094-0-1

Cover Design: Oddball Dsgn
Editor: Lisa DeGloria
Proofreader & Typesetter: Carla M. Dean, U Can Mark My Word

Copies can be ordered by sending $12.00 plus $5.00 for shipping and handling to:

James Tanner Publications
P. O. Box 7206
Silver Spring, MD 20907

Printed in the United States of America by Signature Book Printing, www.sbpbooks.com

STORIES

STORY ONE
THUG DISAPPOINTMENT

The biggest setback among the black race from the time of slavery until this very day we live in is a snitch! I'll never forget my first real run-in with a thug snitch. It was a cold, rainy night in March, somewhere about the year 1982. In my neighborhood, they called me Funky Dunk, and I was a young teenaged Viking who was about to learn the true meaning of "thugism". I didn't have a clue what I was about to get myself into or the direction my life would take. One thing I knew for sure was that I had some bad intentions!

Anyway, I hooked up with a close friend named BAD, who lived on the second floor of the apartment building that I lived in. BAD was the type of person who looked for recognition in any way and anywhere he could. He had to prove himself to everyone. I remember when everyone in the hood would put major pressure on his ass. He was a momma's boy for one, and he was a fat, out-of-shape punk with no heart, and that's just for starters. That's how he earned the nickname BAD, which stands for Bitch-Ass Donnie.

Pointblank, Donnie was a bitch-ass nigga who needed some victims to make a gangster-type name for himself in the hood. He didn't have to prove himself to me, though, because I was his neighbor. It wasn't my role to care about how others viewed him. Plus, he hadn't crossed me yet, so I didn't care.

Somewhere down the line, BAD grew some heart or bought some heart pills from somewhere, because he wanted to go on a mission. I mean a real mission, stick-up boy style. Being that we were both broke as a motherfucker and needed to get our hands on some fast, cold cash, we decided to smoke some Love Boat.

The whole world flipped out of their fucking mind when Love Boat was created. Love Boat was marijuana sprayed with formaldehyde. There were two things that the shit would do to your ass. One, you might find your ass on someone's rooftop without a stitch of clothing on and about to jump to your death. Two, it would give you some false heart and make a bitch-ass nigga a gangster for a couple of hours, which is what happened to BAD.

Anyway, we decided to pull off the fastest way in history to become paid, to do a robbery. After we both were spaced out off the Love Boat, we went on our mission.

"We're gonna get paid!" BAD screamed, with a look of confidence on his face.

I fired up another joint of Love Boat, and after smoking it down about halfway, I passed it to BAD. Slowly, I began to feel the effects.

I should jump out of the window, was my first thought.

"Shhhit! I ain't trippin' that hard," I mumbled to myself.

Holding a 9mm semi-automatic pistol in my hand and having Love Boat in my system, I was definitely ready to take on my part of the mission. BAD, on the other hand, started tripping. I could tell the medication was kicking in on his ass, too, because for the next five minutes, BAD screamed, "I'm Superman, motherfuckers! I'm Superman! I'm Superman, motherfuckers! I'm Superman!" He hollered this while ripping off his size 10X shirt.

"You fakin' 'cause the real Superman could shoot

himself in the head and never get a scratch on him," I said.

BAD looked at me and said, "You're right." Then, he snatched the 9mm pistol out of my hand, put it to his head, clicked the hammer back, and yelled, "Up, up, and away."

Ten seconds passed, as we looked each other straight in the eye.

Suddenly, he burst out laughing. "Nigga, you must really think I'm crazy!"

"No, I don't. I just wanted to see if you were stupid," I replied.

"That's some good shit, but that shit ain't that good!" BAD chuckled.

I laughed, and then I saw our first victims out of the corner of my eye.

There was a frail, white man, a black woman who looked like a hooker, and a big-ass Saint Bernard that looked scared as a motherfucker. We headed toward them, and the closer we got, the more it seemed as if they were preparing for whatever was going to happen.

"Do you have the time?" I asked the white man.

Before the man could reply, BAD pulled out the 9mm pistol and screamed, "Give me every motherfuckin' dime you got in your pocket, white man!"

Shaking like a goddamn leaf, the cracker handed me his wallet. The dog took off like a deer running from a hungry lion, leaving his master and the hooker bitch for dead. The hooker, on the other hand, lifted her short skirt up.

Without a stitch of underwear on, she stretched open her pink pussy lips with both hands and said, "I don't have any money for you to take, but I sure have a pussy that's worth about a million dollars."

I started to take her up on her offer, but instead, I said, "Bitch, this ain't no rape. This is a robbery. Are you crazy?"

BAD and I then ran to a nearby car we had hidden in the cut. I hopped in first, and then seconds later, BAD hopped in and sped off. I told BAD that he did a good job, and I thought he'd be a good stick-up boy if he continued to practice. As for me, Al Capone was my hero, even though he hated niggers. That was cool with me, though, because this wasn't the time to worry about who liked or hated the color of my skin. It was the love and respect I had for a gangster that mattered, and BAD was well on his way, or so I thought.

We began looking for our next victim. We did a bit of driving, and it was about forty minutes before we caught our damn fool. We saw a big, strong-looking black man taking a large box from the trunk of his car. He was dressed very casually in a pair of black slacks, a gray plaid tennis shirt, and a pair of black penny loafers. The man seemed to be an average Joe.

I yelled out to him, “Happy Birthday, big man!”

He smiled and said softly, “It’s not my birthday.”

That’s when BAD smacked him with the pistol. “Get your bitch ass in the car. Better still, which one of these joints you live in?”

Holding the side of his head, the man pointed at a red brick row house in the middle of the block and said, “That one.”

I grabbed the box and we quickly walked him to the house.

Once we got inside, the man cried out, “Y’all don’t have to rob me. I’ll give you my money.”

I looked at BAD, who looked at me, as I hunched my shoulders.

BAD looked at the man and said, “What the fuck you talking about?”

“No, no, no…see, over there I have a box of apples that

I pay guys to throw at me when I'm dressed as a woman. I'm a queen!"

"So you're a fuckin' faggot?" I asked. "How much money do you normally pay people to throw apples at you?"

He pulled out about one thousand dollars and said, "Quite handsomely."

This was no joking matter, but I laughed.

The faggot said, "I'll be one person you won't have to worry about going to the police. Plus, it'll be fun."

BAD screamed at me loud and clear. "I don't believe this shit! So, what the fuck are you thinking about – throwing the motherfuckin' apples at this freak, huh? Is that what you're telling me?"

I looked BAD in the eye and said, "Yeah!"

"I know this is some crazy shit," BAD shouted, "but I'm gonna sit here and watch you throw every one of them apples at his funky ass, man."

I figured the faggot was right. If I threw the apples at him and he paid me for doing that, it wouldn't be a robbery. I threw apple after apple until my entire right arm was numb with pain.

"Ouch! Ooh! Ouch!" the faggot screamed every time I

punished his ass with one of those hard-ass Granny Smith apples. It seemed as if he was having multiple orgasms, or as if someone was straight roddin' him up his ass.

BAD said, while shaking his head, "Man, there are some crazy motherfuckers in this world."

Minutes later, it was time to roll out.

The faggot handed me about a grand and said, "Hold up. I have something I want to show you."

He opened a closet door and pulled out a few metropolitan police shirts, jackets, cuffs, a badge, and even his motherfuckin' gun. That's right, he was the motherfuckin' fed!

"Quick! Tie this motherfucker up!" BAD yelled.

"Wait! No! I only showed you this to say if you ever see me on duty, please never mention this to anyone."

As the gay cop screamed, we continued tying him up until he couldn't raise an eyebrow even if he wanted to. He was crying and slobbering so much, he looked like a rabid dog.

"Shut the fuck up, bitch!" BAD screamed, as he started pacing around the room. "Funky Dunk, we gotta shut this motherfucker up before he gets us caught."

BAD found an iron bat in the closet and beat the guy in the head until both the cop's eyeballs popped out and one ear hung by a single tissue thread. It was a bloody, bloody mess. I stood there stunned.

"Let's get the fuck outta here," BAD said.

Running like two racehorses, we got the fuck out of that joint.

Later that night, after BAD and I separated, I went home and watched the news with my mother. I saw the most interesting story that I'd ever seen on TV; it was a crime that I had helped commit. The feds were saying the suspects had left so many fingerprints that they would easily be able to identify the people who were involved.

About five o'clock the next morning, the police knocked down my mother's door and they meant business. There must have been about five hundred cops in my mother's apartment; she was scared to death. I listened to the feds beat my mother for about ten minutes before they realized she wasn't me. She cried and screamed loud from the pain. They broke her jaw, her nose, and her back. They finally found me between two mattresses, but they didn't do anything to me. I guess they had beaten my mother so badly that they were tired.

When I arrived at police headquarters, BAD was already there. He had turned himself in when he heard the news from his mother. I kept looking at him, trying to catch a clue about how we were going to play this whole thing out. For some reason, though, BAD kept avoiding my eyes.

Before I could say anything to BAD, the police took me into a dark room with a tall lamp that stood about five feet tall. There was a long mirror covering one whole wall. The rest of the walls were painted a shade of green that looked like vomit. As soon as I stepped one foot inside the room, a cracker officer slapped me in the face about a dozen times. I remember him yelling, "Why did you do that shit, nigga? I should kill your black ass!"

"Do what?" I asked.

"You know what the fuck I'm talking about!" the officer yelled back.

He slapped me a few more times, and I knew this cracker would kill me if he could. I held my hand over my head to stop some of the pain.

"Don't put your hand up now, you son of a bitch! What about my officer? How do you think he felt before you niggas killed him?"

"I didn't do nothing!" I hollered desperately.

Three more police officers came into the room and

started beating me, as well. I couldn't take it. I'd never been able to take a good ass whooping.

I have to fight or they will probably kill me, I thought.

I grabbed one officer by his nuts and pulled them so hard he lost his breath. To back it up, I hit him with a jab and a straight right hand across his jaw. The cracker came running across the room as if he was Flash Gordon, but I broke his motherfuckin' nose as soon as he got to me. I snatched his gun when he bent over to hold his bloody face. It was on and poppin' from that point; I had something to work with now.

"Yeah, you bitch-ass motherfuckers!" I screamed, as I started firing the pistol, killing two officers at pointblank range.

The rest of the police officers started running for cover. I took two more pistols from the dead officers that were lying on the floor.

"Come on, you dick eatin' motherfuckers! Y'all think Jason was a motherfucker? Come and get this death I'm giving!"

I could hear gunshots coming from everywhere. Those motherfuckers weren't trying to die. They held court with me, but I wasn't going out like a sucker. I was bustin' right back at their asses!

I started making my way to the door and was hit by a .45 caliber in my left shoulder. It felt like lightning had hit me. I wanted to quit, but it was too late. It was sink or swim. I got myself in this shit, so I had to get out of it.

The feds were firing at me like there was no tomorrow. That's when I had to say my prayers. I prayed as I never prayed before! I wasn't looking for God to get me out of the front door; I just wanted Him to keep them from killing me.

Suddenly, I heard a voice say, "Put your gun down and we won't hurt you!"

My prayers had been answered! God rescheduled my date with death until another time. I threw my guns out in the center of the floor, took off my bloody T-shirt, and waved it in the air.

"Put your hands on your head and stand up!" the police officer screamed.

"I've been shot in the shoulder; I can't put both of my hands up," I responded, while raising my right hand up as high as I could so they could see it.

Luckily, they saw it and didn't kill me. I was taken to DC General Hospital and treated for my gunshot wound.

The next morning, I was taken to the US District Court.

That's when I saw BAD again. I knew something was up with him because he still would not look at me. I was bruised and bloody from my ass kicking, and BAD didn't have one scratch on him. To top it all off, an officer whispered a few words to BAD, then they both looked at me and BAD nodded his head. I wanted to kick his ass, but I was wounded and couldn't break his ass off nothing. It was okay, though, because I knew I would see him again down the line. I didn't know what he told the cops, but I knew it wasn't good.

After a long day in court and many trips from the DC jail to the courthouse, I was broken in. The very thing I never wanted to be I became, and it wasn't hard to get there. I got into a few fights, but for good reasons. The first reason was I needed to earn a reputation, and the second was I had to make every effort to gain an even better reputation for myself. By this time, I couldn't wait to get at BAD, the bitch-ass, hot motherfucker that he was.

I began telling my new friends about BAD and the shit he had done to me. That way, I could make his bit rough for him if any of my new friends ran across him. Funny, I didn't see BAD one time while I was in jail.

Many of my new friends were very well known at the

different prisons in Lorton, Virginia. Lorton had as many as eight different prisons located in its backyard: Occoquan 1, 2, and 3, and Youth Center 1 and 2. There was also Central, Maximum Security, and Minimum Security.

Later that year, I was sentenced to ten years. This dude on my block told me that BAD decided to turn the state's evidence against me in exchange for a lighter sentence for himself. Come to find out, his mother had also watched the news that night BAD had killed the cop. He confessed to his mother about what we had done, and she convinced him to turn himself into the feds so he wouldn't go down by himself. In this case, I learned how fake-ass niggas who were supposed to be gangsters really were, especially when they hit the white man's courtroom and couldn't get off their momma's tit. That's how it is when you're a thug snitch.

Anyway, getting ten years was sweet for me, because I could get back in the street and it would be more sooner than later. With parole, I would be right back on the pound doing it all over again in four years. Plus, my new friends DOODOO, Rick the Killer, Big MOMO, and Chucky the Bumper Car Rapist were all cool. No matter what types of cases they had, it was all cool. They were tough guys who did time most of their young lives in prison from Oak Hill to Cedar Knoll.

A couple weeks after I got my time, I was sent on a Lorton load. My new friends and I kept in close contact with each other on the strength that we were like brothers. Well, more like a mafia organization really. We wrote each other letters through inner-jail mail or we'd send a word through another inmate. Finally, my boys came to Big Lorton. Central was nicknamed The Hill. Dorm 17 was my home, but my partners were still in the intake block. Immediately, I bought my partners three knives each. In Lorton, it's a must that you be strapped, because any and everything happens at Lorton.

One night, Chucky the Bumper Car Rapist, Rick the Killer, and I sat in the back of the rec yard talking about our cases. Chucky was telling us how he would rape his victims, and Rick the Killer told us how he took hits on people who didn't pay their drug debts to drug dealers.

"I'd see a bitch driving alone at night, and my dick would instantly get hard as a rock," Chucky said aggressively. "I know I've raped over 1,900 bitches over the last eight years."

"How did you get them to stop?" I asked.

"Funky Dunk, I would just run into the back of their car and act like it was a mistake. Then I would show them my .44

Magnum, take them to a spot, and fuck 'em. Most of the time, they'd be scared and start crying out that 'Just don't kill me!' shit. I'd usually smack the shit out of them and tell 'em to be quiet. I raped one bitch at least thirty times, and she never called the police. She was in love with this dick. A lot of them bitches like for a nigga to take that pussy."

"You're a crazy motherfucker!" I said, thinking how I was glad he never ran across any of my people because it would've been war. No shit!

Personally, I didn't understand the reason why he would do some crazy shit like that, but the world is big and packed tight with a whole lot of fucked-up people. You just gotta watch your back. That goes for bitches and niggas!

"I ain't into rapin' a bitch, but I will kill a bitch quick!" Rick said. "I used to make about ten thousand dollars a hit, and I don't be bullshittin' when I come get a motherfucker. Man, I'm known everywhere for gettin' my man: Potomac Gardens, The Capers, 37th, East Gate, and Langston Lane."

Rick spoke of the wildest hit job he had ever pulled. "I remember when this nigga paid me to kill this dude. I just walked up to the guy and shot him in the chest three times. I stuck a screwdriver in his head until it came out the other side, then I reached in his pants, cut his dick off, and put it in his mouth. Somebody had to do it, so what the fuck."

Rick kept bragging about the killings and hit jobs he had pulled off. I just sat there and listened as he re-enacted most of his serial-killer profile-type murders. It didn't seem real; it seemed as if he was telling us a horror story.

Early the next morning, Rick got a visit from his girlfriend, who brought him down some pack. In Lorton, "pack" means a package of drugs to sell to other inmates and correctional officers or have for your own personal use. Everybody was doing some hard time down that mickyflick, which is DC slang for a person's location; and they had to be on something in order to get through it.

Anyway, Rick's girlfriend brought ten bundles of heroin that held ten little packages in each bundle. She also had two of her girlfriends bring in an ounce of cocaine each. The three of us - Rick, Chucky, and I - sold the drugs for money, cigarettes, and items from the canteen truck. Over a period of four years, we made about two hundred thousand dollars apiece - that's no bullshit.

The guards would come every now and again to search us for drugs, but we always knew they were coming. The guards who bought drugs from us would tell us when to expect them and how they would be coming. What better motherfuckers to have on our side than a captain, two sergeants, and ten officers.

Money opened a lot of doors for a nigga in Lorton, too, because we started paying the female officers for pussy. We got crazy head and ass from the female correctional officers. In fact, Chucky had three kids by three different female officers. Rick had two kids by one of the captain's daughters. I worked my shit on a couple of correctional bitches, but they started getting on my motherfuckin' nerves, so I just pushed game at the ho's and stepped off. My grandmother always said, "If you can coach a bitch into bumping her motherfuckin' head, send the whore in for a crash landing." I worked those bitches for most of my bit because Lorton was my home and I had to make it as comfortable as possible for me.

******

I heard through the grapevine that BAD was back on the streets and about to get into college. He was always the type of clown who could think of a way to get his ass out of the hot seat quick. I'm not hating on him or anything; I'm just fucked up. I can't get at his bitch ass, but he did some sucker-ass shit to me that needed to be dealt with. If you're a thug, then you know what I'm talking about.

During the mid-summer, my main man, DOODOO, caught a new case on The Hill for stabbing a guy. The word was out that the guy was BAD's cousin, so DOODOO decided to break his ass off something. I heard that DOODOO carved the words "BAD, YOU'RE NEXT!" in the guy's chest with the knife. BAD was sure to get that message.

The captain told Rick, MOMO, Chucky, and me that the guy died on the operating table, and the state of Virginia would be charging DOODOO with murder. I made sure he kept canteen, and the rest of our crew made sure he didn't want for nothing. A few months went by and the state of Virginia did prosecute DOODOO. Murder was the case that they gave him. DOODOO was later sent to a prison in Marion, Illinois. We tried to keep in contact with each other, but the federal system wouldn't accept mail from inmates in other federal correctional facilities.

"DOODOO is a gangster. He ain't got no problem with doing another number," Rick said.

I agreed one hundred percent. DOODOO was all man; no doubt about it.

We sat around for a couple of hours remembering the shit DOODOO did on the compound. It was nothing for DOODOO to go on the small walk, rob somebody, then come back and act as if he ain't do shit. I'm sure he carried it the same way in Marion.

Chucky got into a beef with the southeast crew, which brought a whole lot of good, strong niggas into a situation that could cost them their lives. Chucky got stabbed in the chest, back, neck, and dick about eighteen times. The southeast crew caught him asleep in the dormitory while everyone went to the chow hall to eat.

The one thing you don't do in jail is stay up all night and sleep all fuckin' day. Too much activity goes on during the day. People are moving from dorm to dorm, new niggas are coming on the compound, your enemy is watching for the perfect time to put a knife in your ass, and motherfuckers be stealing and trying to rob a nigga if he's weak. Chucky should've known better than to do a stupid thing like that.

Now this is the fucked up part - one of the Southside niggas claimed Chucky was the one who raped his mother and five-year-old sister. We knew Chucky's track record was taking pussy, and we clearly understood how the dude felt about the situation, so what could we do? Well, some people deserved the shit that came back their way, but in this case, I felt that I needed to do the right thing by putting the knife right back in the niggas who stabbed my partner, even though Chucky was wrong as a motherfucker.

One thing a real thug nigga doesn't do and that's to not handle his business in the time of need, especially when the odds are against him. You got a lot of claim-to-be thugs or gangsters that will leave your ass in a heartbeat. Me, I'm a thug nigga. I always got my man's back. All them fake-ass niggas need to sense is death, and they start running like a bunch of punk-ass pussies.

I kept walking around the prison yard, acting as if I had no beef with the guys who did that shit. A week later, I went and stabbed two of the niggas who played roles in that shit with Chucky. I had MOMO to punish a couple more of them niggas. We realized the position Chucky had put us in just by being his friend, and I was sure other families had the same animosity against him, just as the guy from the Southside. But I had to do the right thing in an otherwise wrong situation.

In life, we run into many types of people, a few good ones and so many bad ones. This is a great big ol' world we live in, and it's packed tight with a whole bunch of shit. If you don't believe me, pick some shit to get into without being conscious of what you're doing and get your ass tore off! That's what the world has to offer you when you're not aware of the situation you have gotten yourself into.

Chucky died on the way to a nearby hospital, and his family sued the Lorton prison system, settling out of court for $100,000. Chucky's life was a big price to pay for such a small amount of money.

After that incident, things got worse for Rick. Forty-four detectives from forty-four different states came to interview Rick and filed charges against him for murder in each state. I haven't heard anything from him since, but I'm sure he has his hands full and is going to handle his business.

I was released to a halfway house about a year later. I got a job at a trash company pulling cardboard out of trash piles that stood about sixty feet tall for recycling purposes. After a while, I got back in the hang of things. I didn't expect a nigga to give me shit, so I made my own way and paid my own way.

The problem with a lot of these so-called thugs, gangstas, and hustlers are they're full of bullshit. They come home from these prisons and think a nigga owes them something because they heard through the grapevine that a nigga doin' good. That's how they end up right back in the penitentiary, trying to track a motherfucker down instead of looking somewhere for a job.

I haven't seen or heard anything from BAD, but I do know one thing for certain and two things for sure; he's on my time and I don't care if it takes twenty years - I will get even!

STORY TWO
THUG GANGSTER BITCHES

It has been said that man will never know his strength until he meets his foe. Well, here she is - the bitch. Ever since the beginning of time, a bitch has been man's biggest foe.

Now there's a big difference between an ordinary bitch and a thug gangster bitch; I'll tell you why. See, the ordinary bitch is the one that thinks her pussy pays the tab for everything. She's the one that uses her pussy as poisonous venom to paralyze a man's mental and physical state of being. On the other hand, the gangster bitch is the one that's gonna make it happen all the way around the board. I mean, support, supply, encourage, have faith, and even kill for her thug if it comes down to it. There's no fakin'; the ordinary bitch ain't going that far. She just wanna fuck you every five minutes and worry you the rest of the day about some goddamn money. I hate a beggin' ass woman!

My name is Kilolo, and I was definitely a thug gangster bitch back in the day. I was a go-hard bitch that would get down and dirty for mine. When I say down and dirty, I mean in the true essence of those words. Back then, I stood about 5'11" and weighed about 160 pounds. I was and still am as black as the tar in the middle of the street, and I have an ass like you've never seen before.

There were three other bitches in my stable that were just as gangsta as me. Shit, we were like family. My partners, Jackie the Hooker, D-Murder, and Six were all a team, especially in the world of crime. Jackie was very good at pretending to be a hooker. She did everything that a professional hooker did except sell her pussy. She was a white girl from a small town in Casper, Montana, and was built like a motherfuckin' sista. I mean, she was all ass and titties. This gangsta bitch was bad. The funny thing about Jackie was she had never seen a black man or woman until she came to Washington, DC.

D-Murder was quiet and very polite. She was a beautiful person inside and out, but she was as cold as Jack the Ripper was to his many victims.

Six was a con artist and the executioner in the group. She was blessed with the gift of gab to talk any person out of some major shit. She was born with three fingers on each hand, which is how she got the nickname Six. Six's mother was a drunk and a crack head, which had a big effect on how Six turned out. As a result, she took her uncontrollable rage out on her victims. Six had to pay a heavy price growing up, but she grew into a vicious and violent gangster bitch.

We were about twenty years old when we pulled the job of a lifetime. One day, Six and I were just sitting around talking and getting high. For some reason, Six was really down and becoming all sentimental and shit. I knew she'd seen her mother that day, but she wouldn't tell me what happened. Six just kept babbling on and on about her childhood.

"I remember when my mother would sit me in front of certain restaurants in Georgetown with a fishbowl, and tell me to ask white people for money. Then she and my stepfather would smoke and drink the money up in crack and alcohol. I used to hate them for that shit! Do you know how embarrassing it was for me as a child to have six fingers and no thumbs? All the other kids had each and every one of their fingers, including their two thumbs," Six said, as she held me tight in her arms for about fifteen seconds with tears rolling down her face and snot coming from her nose. "Kilolo, y'all my family. I have no one else in this world I can trust or count on but y'all. I just hurt so much inside."

Personally, I really didn't know what to say to her because life was just as hard for me, as well. My mother did so much shit to me that I wouldn't know where to start if I were to tell my story.

While I was still sitting with Six, my cell phone rang. It was a friend named Charlie GoGo, who paid us to carry out hits for him. He believed that the truth should always remain in silence, if you know what I mean.

"Hey, you phat, fine, sexy motherfucker," Charlie GoGo said.

"Hey. What's up, baby?" I responded sadly.

"What's wrong with Charlie's angel?"

"I'm just tied up for a minute with Six. She has a few things on her mind that need to be dealt with. Can I call you back?"

"Sure, take ya time. I just wanted to tell you that I have a job for you and the girls to handle for me."

"Okay, I'll call you right back."

A few minutes later, Six pulled herself together and, needless to say, I did, too. It's hard sometimes when you have to be strong for your friend and yourself at the same time, but life is a bitch and the show must go on. Therefore, it was time to put in some work.

I told Six I had somewhere to go, but I really just needed to get away from her crying ass. She was so hard most of the time, but when it came to reminiscing about her mother, it always brought out the baby in Six.

When I got home, I hit Charlie GoGo back, and he told me the deal.

"What's up, Charlie?"

"Hey, what's the deal? You finished with Six? What's wrong with her?" Charlie asked.

"Yeah, we're finished, but what's wrong is none of your business. You know, personal shit," I said.

"All right, that's cool. I didn't wanna talk about that shit anyway. I called for some other shit. Look, there's a nigga doing some crud at my nightclub. That nigga be kidnapping local drug dealers when they leave the club at night. That shit gotta stop 'cause it makes my business look bad. At the same token, niggas might think I'm behind it all. I need you and your girls to take care of that nigga."

"Okay, we'll be by the club tonight. Bye."

After I hung up with Charlie, I called the girls and told them the deal. We agreed to meet up around midnight and head to Charlie's nightclub, Club Atlantis.

Man, he had that place laid out. Charlie was a rich drug dealer and a murderer, but he had a fetish for aquariums. There were fish everywhere – at the three bars, in the bathrooms, and in the VIP. The dance floor was even an aquarium. People danced all night long while looking at exotic fish and eel swimming below their feet. He even had dancers dressed like mermaids. Shit! I guess that was what having millions of dollars could buy.

Charlie met us at the door and walked us to his huge private office. It was like walking into the ocean. All of the walls were glass with fish and shit swimming around. He always kept the lights dimmed so it would look like we were underwater. Being inside his club always made me nervous. If someone shot up the place, people would be running from the bullets *and* those damn eels.

As usual, Charlie showed his appreciation by doing one thing that was well respected between each and every one of us. Charlie always had a bottle of Louis the XIII for us to drink because he knew a woman intoxicated off a bottle of that shit could do some major damage, one way or the other. He then rolled up some of the best weed I had ever had. He showed us the bamma that was doing the crud and we got right on top of that.

I played the "clown" like a real bozo, and that made our job a lot easier. D-Murder and I walked up to the guy. We decided that I would play the shy role at first, so she did all of the talking.

"If it's okay with you, my girlfriend wants to buy you a drink," D-Murder said.

"Um, okay," he said, as he looked around the room nervously.

"You don't have to get paranoid or anything. She's a beautiful black woman in search of a strong, courageous man. Do you think you can handle a strong woman like that?" D-Murder was laying that flirting shit on thick.

"Young lady, you don't know who you're talking to. I'm

that nigga that you take home to Mom and tell her, 'He's the one!'"

We laughed as if we were laughing with him, but that shit was corny. I wanted to kill this motherfucker on the spot for saying some dumb shit like that.

"So, what's your name?" D-Murder asked.

"Butch Bang," he said to me, as I thought the name really described what we were gonna do to the cruddy motherfucker.

"My name is Laverne and my girlfriend's name is Shirley," D-Murder said.

I held out my hand toward him and gave him a sly and seductive smile.

"Hello, beautiful," he said.

"Shirley, meet Butch Bang," D-Murder said quietly.

After the short introduction, D-Murder left me alone with Butch Bang to do what I do best; play the bamma out of his life. I saw my girls watching us from a dark corner of the nightclub, as Butch Bang and I got closer and closer during the night. Drink after drink and dance after dance, we cuddled the night away. I could tell D-Murder and Six were mad because I was taking a long time with Butch Bang.

Finally, Charlie GoGo was ready to close the club and there was no sign of Butch Bang or me. The girls told me later that they figured Butch Bang might have talked me out of the plan and my panties. Little did they know they were right. Well, partially right.

The next morning, I called Jackie to see what was up.

"Did you take care of that nigga, Butch Bang?" Jackie asked.

"No. The opportunity never came up, Jackie." I knew that shit sounded like a lie, but I had to roll with it.

"What? Bitch, you should've taken care of that last night. You know how important this is to Charlie GoGo. I'm fucked up at you, Kilolo. I just wanna ask you one question."

"What's that?"

"Did you fuck that man?"

"Hell, no! Come on, you know I don't roll like that. What kinda bitch you take me for?"

Actually, I did fuck him, but I didn't want to admit it. All I could think about was his touch and the way he held onto me when we were dancing. It was something I wanted for a long time. Don't get me wrong. I'm a gangster bitch and would go hard as a motherfucker, but I was still a woman and definitely needed love.

After we ditched the club, we went to a hotel around the corner. He slid his thick-ass, big, black, twelve and a half inch dick in and out of my wet, tight pussy all night long. Damn, he made my pussy cum about twenty times. I sucked his dick for about an hour before he even fucked me. It sure was a long time since I had some action like that. The first thing I said to myself when I woke up was, “Aw shit, I’m in trouble now.” I had to admit it. Butch Bang had a big ol’, fat, black dick and I was in love with it.

Anyway, Jackie continued her cross-examination of me, but I didn’t tell her nothing. I just felt guilty as a motherfucker inside because I lied to her, and that meant I crossed her and the rest of the girls, as well, which was not cool. That was some sucker-ass shit I did, crossing them for a dick, or should I say a nigga that really was supposed to be dead the second after I fucked him.

“Kilolo, you need to get your ass over here. We gotta figure out what to do.”

“Fine. I’ll be there in an hour.”

When I got to Jackie’s place, the girls were sitting around and smoking a blunt. Jackie was my girl, but she kept a nasty house. Every time I went to her house, I looked at the same trash on the floor. There were always dishes piled high in the sink. I only went in her bathroom once because it was so damn nasty. The toilet had pee stains and hair all over the seat, and the tub had one-inch thick grime around it. To top it all off, her place smelled like a baby's shitty diaper, even though she had no kids.

After smoking for a little while, I told Jackie and the rest of the girls that when we left the club, Butch Bang took me through a couple of the neighborhoods where he sells his drugs. That's not what happened though. I was lying to them, trying to make it seem as if I was on point. If they knew I was lying to them, they would have killed me for sure. We were "sisters," but we pledged death to a sellout, especially one of our own.

I drove them through a few drug strips to make it seem real, and I even picked out a house and told them his mother lived there. To be honest, the only two things I really knew about Butch Bang was that he had a big dick and I wanted some more.

I didn't expect what happened next. Six and D-Murder were real eager for some action.

"Let's park this shit right here. If Butch comes out, we'll blast his ass," Six said.

"Yeah, that nigga gotta pay for all the shit he done."

Six and D-Murder got out of the car when someone came out of the house. D-Murder pulled out a .45 automatic handgun and shot the first person she saw, which happened to be a child that looked no older than four years old. I felt bad only for a moment, and then it didn't matter because I killed people for a living anyway. What the fuck? The child probably would have grown up to be some shit anyway.

D-Murder and Six continued to shoot every person that came out that door. All I could hear was screaming and crying. *Please don't shoot me! Oh, my God!*

By the time the shooting stopped, there was a pile of dead motherfuckers all over the street. There had to be about ten bodies in the yard and in the street. A couple of people tried to run after being shot, so there were blood trails on the sidewalk. There was even one woman holding her baby. Six shot the woman in her head, but the baby was still alive.

Upon hearing sirens, we jumped in the car and rolled out. I knew the situation was turning into some sucker shit, but once you tell one lie, you gotta tell another one and another one and another one.

Later that night, I was in bed trying to go to sleep. Just as I drifted off, Charlie GoGo called my cell phone.

"Hello," I answered sluggishly.

"Hey, what's up with the mission I sent y'all on? This motherfucker is still doin' the same shit."

It sounded as if he was mad as hell, and he had every right to be. The business wasn't taken care of, and on top of it all, I was in love with a dead man walking. Charlie GoGo told me about another kidnapping Butch Bang had pulled. I knew the girls and I had to do something about the situation, but I just didn't know what.

"I was told that Butch Bang and a couple of his friends kidnapped two guys at gunpoint that work for me at my nightclub. Butch and those niggas pulled both of the guys' eyeballs out of their heads after they gave up my money. It's gonna be a Judgment Day for that motherfucker now. I got seventy-five thousand dollars on that nigga's head. Can y'all take care of that, Kilolo?"

"Sure. We'll take care of that fool."

"Cool," Charlie GoGo slowly said.

After I got off the telephone with Charlie GoGo, I called

the girls to tell them what the deal was. It was time to set that bamma up, no doubt about it. I had to put aside my feelings or I'd mess up the whole thing.

We played the club scene for weeks, and there was no sign of Butch Bang anywhere. The girls had a problem with the fact that I could've gotten him the first time, but I told them that it wasn't the right time.

"Look, y'all, all this bickering and shit ain't gonna get it. Plus, there's more money on this nigga's head this time."

Deep down inside, I didn't mean a word I said to them. All I knew was I was in love, and if he was gonna be dead, his dick would be dead right in my mouth.

Eventually, I caught up with Butch Bang at a nearby Blockbuster movie rental store. I was driving around one day and saw him standing outside of the door as if he was waiting on someone. I parked and walked up to him. I spoke to him softly, as my heart pounded harder and harder while we stood close.

"Hello, Butch Bang."

He looked around as if he saw himself on America's Most Wanted or something. "Bitch, don't ever call my name out loud like that," he replied quietly. "Now, who in the hell are you?"

I was so hurt inside. It felt like someone ripped my heart right out of my chest along with my feelings. I just walked away and cried.

A few seconds later, he caught up to me. "I'm totally sorry for my rudeness, but I don't quite remember where I know you from."

"I met you just over a month ago at Club Atlantis. My girlfriend introduced us. My name is Shirley."

"Oh yeah, I remember you now. I stole that money out of your pocketbook, right? Or are you the one who I sold your little sister's baby to them country white motherfuckers from that small town in Ohio?"

"No, I'm not either one of them."

A few seconds later, this long-legged bitch walked up and stood beside him. "Who's this?" she asked.

"Baby, I don't know who this bitch is. She just asked me for some change," he said, then walked off.

She looked me up and down, and then she walked off, as well.

I couldn't believe he played me like that. Even though I knew this bamma had to get it, I still wanted to fuck him just one last time. Before he and the bitch got out of my sight, I ran over to a gold-colored Lexus truck he and the ho got in.

"Hold up, man. Do you wanna rob this nigga for forty pounds of pure cocaine?"

He looked at me with a sincere look of hunger. "How can I get in touch with you?"

I knew I had him! He just got tricked. The hunter was captured by the game. I told him to give me a number where I could reach him, and he gave me his cell phone number, which I called a few times each day just to make him comfortable. Eventually, I would put my fork in his ass, because this nigga was done. Not only was he a foul-ass nigga, but he embarrassed the shit out of me, too. He had to pay.

My plot was as deadly as a blind man swimming through a swamp full of crocodiles. I called the girls and told them just how we were gonna get our victim. Sure, I did plan on fucking him one more time, but there would be a big difference. I was going to really fuck him this time!

I told Jackie, Six, and my girl D-Murder to get all the pistols together because it was time for that motherfucker to pay for his actions. Everybody must be paid back in return for the shit they do in life. When you do good things in life, most of the time, it comes back to you. On the other hand, when you do that crud, it comes back ninety-nine percent harder.

The girls met me at a nearby hotel on New York Avenue. We all got strapped up with the heat and I gave the sucker a call.

"Hey, baby. Are you ready to go on that mission I told you about?" I asked softly.

"Shirley?" he asked in a very low tone. "Yeah, what's up?"

"It's that time; I've been tailing this mock all night."

"Where are you?" he asked.

"I'm on New York Avenue in front of the Motel 8. How fast can you get here?"

"I can get there in five minutes," he replied.

A few minutes passed and sho nuff the dead man walking showed up.

"There he is!" Six screamed out.

"That bitch-ass motherfucker," Jackle said.

"Be cool; let me go and get that nigga," I told them.

I got out of the car and hugged him as he kissed me on my left cheek. I told Butch Bang that I was following the nigga all night to make the story seem real. I also told him to sit with the girls until I finished talking to the clerk at the front desk. I used a fake ID I found at a strip club just in case the cops came around. Once I got the room, I told Butch Bang and the girls to follow me. After opening the door, I walked in. Butch Bang walked in behind me, and the girls were behind him.

"Where is the nigga?" Butch Bang asked.

Before he could say anything else, I pulled out a .38 special and the rest of the shit became history. I shot the nigga four times in the face, and the girls shot him until all their guns were empty. We knew what to do with the body because we did something similar before.

I drove to a nearby hardware store and bought four axes. I purchased one hundred cans of dog food and some trash bags from the grocery store. Then I picked up four ponchos, goggles, and galoshes.

When I got back to the hotel, we all took turns chopping his ass up into little tiny bits and pieces. From his head to his toes, we chopped and chopped for hours. Blood splattered all over the place. The floor was so wet that it felt like we were splashing through rain puddles. Body parts were thrown all over the room; it looked like a scene from the X-Files. By the time we finished, we looked like that girl Carrie from that Stephen King movie.

Finally, it was time to bag him up and take him to a place where we could boil him into a soup. There was an old warehouse in Northeast where we used to hang, so we took him there. We boiled his ass for two hours, and boy did his dead body stink.

To get rid of the evidence, the girls and I opened every can of dog food and mixed them with his body parts. We fed his ass to every dog, cat, and rat in Washington, DC. Then we dumped everything else in the Potomac and drove home.

Now was that the ultimate shit or what? I told you we were thug gangster bitches, didn't I?

STORY THREE
THUG SET-UP

In the summer of 1985, I met a dude named Whispers. He was a real cool cat who knew all the right moves to get paid. Whispers was clean-cut, smart, and spoke very intelligently. He was a small, thin, brown-skinned dude that looked as if he had some Cuban in his blood. I really learned to admire and respect him for a lot of things, until he showed me his trump card.

The slums of New York City were his hometown, but Whispers moved around a lot. As time passed and I got to know him better, I clearly understood why. About 9:45 A.M., I knocked on a door in Washington, DC's upper-class neighborhood, Georgetown. For some reason, this house looked to be a payday for me. I also figured that the owner would be out of town. I knocked for about ten minutes and no one answered. Without any money in my pockets and hunger pains hurting my stomach, that was enough drive to investigate.

I broke into the house through the basement window by using a 2x4 piece of wood to break the metal bars from the windowsill. Next, I made a hole in the window so I could unlock the window and climb into the house. When I got inside, I heard no movement at all.

"Great!" I said with a severe feeling of happiness.

I was so hungry I didn't know whether to rob the house or cook something to eat.

I looked the house over and it seemed as if no one had been there for days. So, I kindly made myself at home by placing the large plate of food, which I had found neatly placed inside the refrigerator, into the microwave oven.

"Wow, turkey wings with rice, gravy, and macaroni and cheese. My favorite dish!" I screamed.

I sat down at the table and started knocking that shit down. I was eating as if I hadn't eaten in weeks. A few minutes later, I fell fast asleep. I was full, comfortable, and restless. I must have slept for at least an hour, only to be awakened by three drooling pit bulls. Suddenly, I felt a thrust full of pain like someone had just punched me in the jaw hard as hell, followed by a flash of light.

Holding the side of my face, I looked up, and there I saw a man who said, “Hello, my name is Whispers. What’s yours?”

I jumped up and ran for the door, but the pit bulls weren’t having it. They bit the shit out of my ass. One of them held me down by the neck with his head, making it hard for me to breathe at all. Whispers called them off me, as he told me to lay face down on the floor while he handcuffed my feet and wrists.

He then pulled out a .357 Magnum, put it to my head, and said, “Let’s try this again. What’s your name?”

I said, “I’m Jason, sir.”

“Don’t ‘sir’ me, motherfucker. Now, what the fuck are you doing in my house?”

“I was hungry,” I replied nervously, my voice shaking and sounding feeble.

“So you broke into my house because you were hungry?”

I was scared as hell when he put the barrel of that gun to the back of my head. To make matters worse, I heard him click the hammer backward.

"Please, Mr. Whispers, please don't kill me. I'm begging you, please."

He slowly moved the .357 Magnum from the back of my head and said, "I'm not going to kill you and neither am I going to call the police. I, my new friend, will put you into my very own plans."

Whispers took the handcuffs off me and began to tell me about his plans and the things we could accomplish together. Whispers told me to come back in a week; he also gave me three hundred dollars to keep me straight until I came back.

A week later, I returned and noticed an envelope with my name on it attached to the screen door. Inside the envelope was the following note:

Dear Jason,

My next-door neighbor has a spare key for you to let yourself in the house. Don't worry about the dogs; they are trained to attack only on command. My girlfriend, Kitten, will be coming to the house, so relax, lie back, or cook a meal and wait for her.

Sincerely,
Whispers

I did exactly what he said. I got the key, let myself in the house, and made a nice, big lobster tail stuffed with shrimp and crab imperial, washing it down with a shot of Cristal champagne.

Finally, Kitten came into the house at about 3:45 A.M. From the smell of her clothes, she had been around a lot of smoke, and from the smell of her breath, she had been drinking a lot of alcohol. She was good and drunk.

I was lying on the couch with one eye open and one eye closed, when all of a sudden, Kitten fell on top of me. As I was lying there, she grabbed my crotch and began feeling for my big, thick, eleven and a half inch, redheaded dick. I laid there without a sound, as she put my dick straight into her warm mouth. About sixty seconds later, I exploded a huge load in her mouth, causing her to choke and begin coughing and gasping for air.

"Are you okay?" I asked.

She answered me with an unconscious statement. "Yes, I think so."

And in an instant, she was fast asleep.

I looked down at her and saw that she had in no way swallowed the load of semen I shot off in her mouth. As it dripped from her mouth like a raw egg, I wiped the thick load from her lips with the end of her dress.

When daylight arose, I made sure that I got up before she did. I didn't know if or when Whispers would show up, so I figured it was the right thing to do.

"Ouch! My head is killing me!" she cried out.

"You had a good time wherever you came from this morning," I said.

"Who are you?" she asked in a very high tone voice.

"Oh, I'm Jason, a friend of Whispers. We met a few days ago. Here are some pain relievers for your headache," I replied.

"Thank you so much," she said, as she gifted me with a smile.

Kitten lay back on the couch with both hands on her head, as I made a glass of tomato juice for her to settle her stomach.

I must admit that Kitten was a very beautiful woman. She stood about 5'11" and weighed about 150 pounds, with an hourglass figure and olive complexion. Kitten was all tits and ass with a beautiful face.

Whispers called to make sure everything was all right, and I told him that Kitten was a little sick, but she'd be okay. He knew immediately that she had been drinking, and he asked me to keep an eye on her while he was not around.

Whispers said, "I hope it doesn't take something tragic to happen in order for her to learn a lesson. Besides, she does things that she shouldn't do when she's drunk."

I knew right then that I would be taking advantage of Kitten every chance I got, because pussy is pussy no matter who it belongs to, and for the most part, she was a hustler and could suck a mean dick, too.

As Kitten started getting herself together, she began telling me about this old guy from Egypt who sells precious diamonds and rubies to merchants in Georgetown. She told me that the old man had many stores in New York, and he made millions doing most of his business with people of celebrity status. The minute she said millions, I was ready to put in some work right then and there. Moreover, I was ready to kill the world because there was so much shit going on in this world that taking another man's shit was the only way I could make a living or make something happen for myself.

I walked to the kitchen to get more Cristal, and Kitten yelled out, "On Monday, the old man will be in town and we need to go get that shit up off of him, you feel me?"

"Yeah, I feel you, but how are we going to get him?" I asked with suspicion.

Kitten replied, "Ain't no 'I' in 'we'. You gonna handle that, slim. I will show you our victim and the rest is on you. I'll tell you another thing; you better not fuck the move up!"

She looked in my eyes with a cold look of death. I didn't trip, though. I just figured I'd use that look as my strength.

Monday rolled around and the old man was right where he was supposed to be.

I walked up beside him and asked, "What time of day is it?"

As he looked at his watch, I made sure it would be the last time he'd ever see a watch again, not to mention tell someone the time of day! I stabbed him in the chest with a bone knife, and then I shot him in the head five times with Whispers' .357 Magnum. I snatched the briefcase filled with the jewels and ran as fast as I could to the getaway car. I handled my business and it went as planned.

After getting back to Whispers' crib, we broke that shit down.

"I can roll with a nigga like you," Kitten said. "I was a little bit leery about you at first, but you came through like a true champion." Kitten also added, "They usually book a flight to Las Vegas to sell the jewelry, but they have someone on this side of the coast to purchase the jewelry. I would've enjoyed a getaway from the hood, but I'm cool with the fact that we got paid."

When Whispers finally got home, we definitely had a nice lump sum of cash waiting for him.

"Surprise!" Kitten said.

When Whispers walked in the house, Kitten hugged and kissed him, while handing him a stack of money.

I smiled and greeted Whispers with nothing but respect. As he shook my hand, he asked how everything went. I said everything was everything.

Whispers looked at me, smiled, and then said, "Jason, welcome to my team. Everything will work out fine as long as you are honest and loyal to us."

I felt as if I were taken in like a stray dog. It was all right with me, though, because all I could see was growth and cash at the end of the rainbow.

We all went out for a bite to eat at the Cheesecake Factory, and afterward, Whispers and I stopped in Saks for Men and bought a few pieces of clothing. Whispers told me to remember that if I didn't belong somewhere, always look like I did belong there!

Kitten began telling Whispers and me how good we looked in the clothes we were trying on in the store. I was overjoyed at the fact that no one ever cared enough to tell me just how good I looked before. In fact, no one ever cared anything about me, not even my parents.

When Kitten stepped off to the ladies' room, Whispers pulled me to the side.

"Jason, I'm a very sick man. I don't think I'll live very long." He went on to explain to me that two years ago he found out that he suffers from prostate cancer, which had spread severely. "Because time is of the essence, I want to enjoy the rest of my life to the fullest, and anything I can do to get paid or get ahead in the game is totally necessary."

Before I could respond, Kitten walked up and hugged

both of us. "A hug for the two important men in my life."

Whispers then began telling Kitten and me about something else he had planned, as we left Saks and drove off.

When we reached Alabama Avenue SE, in Washington, DC, Whispers yelled out of the window at a dark-skinned guy, "Black Mike! Hey, Black Mike!"

After Black Mike came to the car, Whispers asked him for some money he owed him. Suddenly, an argument broke out between them. Whispers got so angry that he got out of the car and stabbed Black Mike in the throat eight times. Then, he pulled Black Mike's pants and underwear down and began stabbing him directly in his asshole about twenty more times until blood was all over the place.

People were screaming and yelling and children were crying as we pulled off. After some serious investigating, we found out a few days later that Black Mike was in the intensive care unit at Washington Hospital Center. Whispers made a call to Black Mike's hospital room, where his grandmother answered the telephone.

"Hello, is Black Mike around?" Whispers asked.

She told Whispers that Black Mike was unconscious and could not talk to anyone. That's when Whispers told Black

Mike's grandmother that Black Mike owed him some money, but since he couldn't talk at the moment, he would make sure that Black Mike never talked again.

Whispers looked at me and said, "Jason, I want you to go into Black Mike's hospital room and pull the life support plug from the machine that he's breathing from."

That same day, I waited for a few hours until his family left the hospital and pulled the plug. He was a done deal!

Later that day, Kitten found out that her mother had fallen ill, and she decided to go spend some time with her. Whispers and I decided to take a trip to the sandy shores of the Bahamas to chill out and see a new atmosphere for a change. At that point, I had never been anywhere in my entire life, so you know I wanted to be with that move.

A few days later, Whispers and I pulled up in front of the Nations Bank on 8th and H Street, NE at about ten o'clock in the morning. One of Whispers' friends had put us on to a multi-millionaire's wife who was about to make a large withdrawal of money from the bank.

She showed up as scheduled and entered the bank. Twenty minutes later, she came out with a big green duffel bag filled with loot. A DC police officer walked her out of the door to an awaiting police patrol car. Two police officers got out and greeted the millionaire's wife, as she handed one of them the duffel bag full of money.

"Good morning, ma'am," the police officer said, as she got into the backseat of the police car.

They began talking as they pulled off. I think she was giving them directions to her home, because I could see her pointing her finger toward Florida Avenue. We tailed them for about half an hour through traffic until they stopped at her home in Sterling, Virginia. The millionaire's wife got out of the police car, and one of the police officers escorted her to the front door with her bag of money.

Whispers and I sat in the car until both officers left, and then Whispers said, "Let's get that money."

I rang the doorbell, while Whispers stood to the left side of the door.

"Good morning, sir. May I help you?" the butler said.

"Good morning," Whispers said. "My son and I are lost. We need to use a telephone. Could you help us so kindly?"

The butler said, "Wait just a second, please."

When he returned, he invited us in to use the telephone. Whispers pretended as if he was dialing a telephone number. I personally kept in mind that there was a large sum of money in the house and I wanted it.

Swiftly, Whispers pulled out his sawed-off shotgun, as I put the .357 Magnum to the butler's head.

"Where is the bitch with all the money?" Whispers yelled out.

"Sir, I don't know what you're talking about."

Whispers put the sawed-off shotgun to the butler's throat and said, "You don't know what I'm talking about, huh? Well, let me help you out a little bit. A bitch came in here from the bank about ten minutes ago with a duffel bag full of money, and if you don't tell me where she is, in a fuckin' casket you will go. You understand?!"

"Yes, sir. Yes, sir," the butler uttered, as he pointed to the stairs.

As Whispers and I headed for the stairs, a house cleaner walked out of a nearby room. I put the .357 to her head, clicked the hammer back, and said, "Lead me to the owners of this house!"

When she saw the handgun in my hand, her eyes opened as wide as two silver dollars. She was scared as a motherfucker. The house cleaner and the butler told us that it would be best if one of them called the owners' bedroom from the kitchen telephone.

Whispers had doubts about that at first, but then he went along with it.

Calmly, Whispers said to me, "When the millionaire's wife comes down to the kitchen, shoot the butler in the head to show her that we mean business."

I nodded my head with an 'I got that' gesture.

The housecleaner called the millionaire's wife. She came straight to the kitchen and Whispers told her what was going on. She didn't understand at first, so I shot the butler in the forehead at pointblank range.

"I think you get the point now, or don't you?" Whispers asked.

When the millionaire's wife said, "Oh, my God, what do you want," I felt like we were getting somewhere. Jason was my name and taking money was my game.

"Bitch, where is that money you got from the bank this morning?" I said.

"It's in the safe upstairs," she cried.

Whispers slapped the millionaire's wife with the shotgun and said, "Bitch, take us to the money."

With her legs shaking and her voice cracking, I could clearly see she was as scared as a child in the dark. I knew we were moments from getting that cheese up off her.

We all went upstairs, where she removed a big picture off the wall. Behind it was a large safe.

"Bitch, hurry up and get that money!" Whispers shouted. "Open the motherfuckin' safe now!"

When she got the safe open, not only did we see stacks and stacks of money, to our surprise, we saw diamonds, rubies, gold bars, and all types of foreign money. Now, I never was the type to underestimate what my hand called for, but this for sure was a class act.

We got everything out of the safe, tied the housecleaner and the millionaire's wife up, and left as quickly as possible.

When we got back to the house, Whispers and I looked over everything and put something for Kitten to the side, but our main focus was making the right moves with the large sum of cash. Whispers asked me if I wanted to go half on 300 kilograms of cocaine. It wasn't a bad idea. However, I wanted to know who would be the one doing most of the footwork, because personally, I didn't want any part of that. If I'm gonna do something to get fifty years, I might as well go straight for the money; fuck selling drugs.

"Jason, we won't go wrong if we bought 300 kilograms of pure cocaine to keep something going for us. In the game, you'll always need to keep something moving or something to move when things get slow."

Even though my chest was flooded with the feeling of achievement already, and despite the fact that I had done something wrong to get paid, I agreed. The thought "what's right in America when it comes to getting paid" came to my mind, and I clearly saw that anything goes.

Whispers and I took off to Nassau, Bahamas. It took us about two and a half hours to get there from Baltimore Washington International.

"The Bahamas is a beautiful place. There are sunshine, blue skies, and clear waters. It really would've been nice if Kitten could've come along with us because she never got the chance to come here. She loves the islands," Whispers said.

I ventured off in thought and imagined Kitten and I were all alone on the beach. Out of my pocket, I pulled a long white candle, stuck it deep into the sand, and lit it, as we sat and had a sexy candlelight beach dinner. I saw myself moving the thin string of her thong swimsuit to the side that separated her pussy from the earth and started giving her all tongue in her naked pussy until she went into convulsions. I just couldn't help it. Every time I thought about her, I thought about her pretty pink-colored lips going back and forth on my big, thick, long dick. I knew I would have her all to myself someday, but for now, I needed to concentrate on getting paid.

Later that night, Whispers and I went to a nightclub called The Zoo. In the Bahamas, The Zoo is a very well-known nightclub. The people are cool and the drinks are off the motherfuckin' hook.

Whispers met this female named Zanzabar in the club. She told us that she was from New York City, the big city of dreams. She stood about 5'6" and weighed about 135 pounds. Zanzabar had long black hair down to her back, with the ass of a horse. She had a brown complexion, with pearly white teeth and a southern accent.

Whispers took her to the hotel room and screwed her from 3:30 A.M. until about 10:00 A.M. When she finally got herself together, she started telling Whispers how good he had fucked her and that she needed to keep in touch with him for that reason. So, they both traded telephone numbers and promised to add each other to their hot list.

"I am so scared, Whispers," Zanzabar said, as she held her head with both hands.

Whispers walked across the room, hugged her, and asked, "What's the problem? What's wrong?"

"I didn't tell you, but I'm a married woman and I haven't seen my husband since I left our hotel room last night to go to the club. We're on our honeymoon. I just got married two days ago."

"Holy shit, you're a ho! Bitch, you ain't nothing but a freak-ass, cheatin'-ass, stankin'-ass ho!" Whispers yelled at her.

She had a real fucked-up look on her face when Whispers got finished cussing her freak ass out. She was fucked up about that, and on top of it all, she was worried to death about what she would tell her newfound husband about her whereabouts after the club.

Whispers decided to dog the bitch because she had proven to be untrustworthy and a sellout.

"When you pledge to take care of a woman for the rest of her life and she fucks a nigga twenty-four hours later that she doesn't even know, she needs to be carried worse than a rat," Whispers quietly whispered to me.

"Zanzabar, I want you to suck Jason's dick," Whispers said.

Without asking any questions, Zanzabar hopped on my dick like a duck on a June bug. She sucked and sucked and sucked for about twenty minutes.

"Um," I moaned, as Zanzabar went up and down my dick from the top of the red head to the bottom of my big nut sac.

She took my dick out of her mouth and smacked it against her face, while she grabbed and started jerking it with a tight grip back and forth.

"I'm getting ready to cum!" I screamed out, as my body began to tighten up.

"No, not yet. Hold it for a while. I want it up my ass," Zanzabar said.

She squeezed the head of my dick grip-lock tight so that a drop of cum could not escape. Then she turned around and opened both of her ass cheeks wide with both hands for me to enter. As I spit in the round hole of her ass and slid my dick up in her, I could feel and hear the hair ripping and tearing from the skin of her ass.

"Oh shit! Oh shit, that dick feels so good in my ass,

Jason," Zanzabar moaned out.

I fucked her up the ass for another forty-two minutes, and then I started cumming.

"Damn, you got some good ass! Damn, you got some good fuckin' ass!" I screamed, as I began to cum inside her ass, and I didn't stop until I felt every drop of my hot cum shoot in the hole of her big phat ass. "Damn! That was good," I said.

Zanzabar opened both of her ass cheeks wide again. When I pulled my dick from her asshole, I couldn't help but to notice a yellow kernel of corn on the head of my dick, surrounded with blood and green shit.

"I see you ate corn before you went to the club last night, huh?" I said.

As Zanzabar looked down at my dick and smiled, I told Whispers to tell that bitch to get missin'.

"Get to steppin', bitch! Get missin' in action!" Whispers yelled out at the hooker.

After the bitch left, Whispers and I went on the party boat, which is a huge boat where men and women get together and do nothing but party, drink, and mingle all day and night. It's filled with fun and adventure. The biggest challenge is to lay your mack down on the lovely ladies while you enjoy the activities onboard.

Everything went fine. I enjoyed myself and Whispers did, as well. We both met some honeys, and we were back on a fuck mission. I met a fine female named Candy, which I nicknamed “The Bahama Momma”, and Whispers hooked up with her girlfriend Sweet Nancy. I gave Sweet Nancy the nickname “Nasty” because everything about her seemed to be nasty. In her conversation, everything was about dick, butt, or pussy, and if it wasn’t that, it was about sucking or fucking. For the moment, I was okay with that, because I wanted to get a nut off in the bitches and be on my motherfuckin’ way.

In my conversation with Candy, I got down to business and asked for the pussy. She agreed to have sex and we went to work. Whispers and I raced those bitches back to the hotel room like a pair of Kentucky Derby racehorses. We wanted to fuck and they did, too.

The moment the room door opened was the moment the fucking, sucking, and licking got started. I jumped out of my clothes and into Candy’s ass like some Good-n-Plenty candy. We humped from room to room, from position to position. I had never experienced getting my asshole licked before and never had I ever licked anyone’s asshole, but this night I was totally broke in. Candy was one fuck I'll never forget. I don't know what went down with Whispers and Nasty, but I can sure imagine that he handled his business.

The next morning, our plane was scheduled to leave the Bahamas at 12:30 P.M. and it was fast approaching 10:00 A.M. We swapped telephone numbers with Candy and Nasty, and then we sent them on their way. We made it to the airport by noon and were ready to get back to Washington, DC.

For some reason, bad feelings started to come over me, and my gut feelings felt insecure about something I just couldn't put my finger on. I didn't know whether I should feel inquisitive or be paranoid. I knew one thing; it didn't sit well with me, and my street instincts told me to watch my back.

During the whole flight back, Whispers told me a few stories about past situations that took place during a certain era of time. I was all ears; in fact, I listened so closely that I heard the shit he wasn't saying. He told me about this guy he killed to take over a certain neighborhood in DC. He mentioned that the guy sold drugs for him and made about twenty thousand dollars a week, which Whispers felt that the twenty grand could go in his pocket if he got rid of the guy. Plus, the runners would work for him, as well.

"The youngin' was my partner and he really trusted me, but I crossed him for the sweet love of money," Whispers said.

As he looked out the corner of his eyes at other people on the aircraft, I thought about things my grandmother used to tell me about trust when it comes to people. She would always tell me never to trust them ol' shifty-eyed motherfuckers or a person that never looks you straight in the eye. I had a close friend named Smallwood that I thought was my best friend in this world, but as it turned out, he was the closest enemy I had in this world. He did some fucked-up shit to me, and it took some time for me to get over it, but he will get his someday. He was the prime example of the kind of people she would talk about, a shifty-eyed motherfucker. My grandmother couldn't stand the bitch-ass nigga; now I understood why.

"I had to cut the middle man out of the picture. I say fuck any nigga that's gonna cut me short," Whispers said in a low tone.

I must say, I felt a little intimidated. I also felt that from here on out Whispers was not to be trusted. Maybe it was the reason I had those bad vibes earlier.

"I called my young partner late one night and told him that I needed him to keep fifteen kilos of cocaine for me. I pulled up in front of his mother's house, and sho nuff, he was on the front porch. I called him to the car and shot him straight in the forehead with a double barrel sawed-off shotgun." Whispers said.

One thing about Whispers; he was the type of person that could never look you straight in the eye. He would look at the ground or plain look in another direction, and I definitely knew what that meant. Grandma also said, "Always recognize what your gut feelings tell you. They will never let you down."

We arrived back in Washington, DC about 3:20 P.M., and we caught a cab back to Whispers' place. The moment we got in the door, we noticed that the house was a total wreck. The dog tore the place apart. After helping Whispers clean up, I left a few moments later.

A few days passed and I dropped by Whispers' house to see what was going on with him. He told me that Kitten was on her way and they had plans to chill out together. I respected that to the utmost, but it seemed to be a little fishy to me, so I moved on.

I stopped at Uno's in Union Station for some drinks, and it was crowded as hell. I mean some shoulder-to-shoulder type of shit. You would have thought Bernie Mac or Cedric the

Entertainer was there. I sat there for about three hours, and guess who walked in the door? Whispers and Kitten were seated right next to my table.

I said, "Excuse me, sir. I can't help but notice that you have a very fine young lady with you."

Kitten smiled from ear to ear.

"I just can't get away from you, Jason," Whispers replied.

"It seems to me that I can't get away from you. I was here first," I said.

Whispers started telling us about another move he had lined up. The whole time he was talking, Kitten was winking her eyes and blowing kisses at me. I tried my best not to look at her, especially when Whispers almost caught her in action.

"My cousin Troy has hit the lottery for $300,000, and the winning ticket is in his house. The plan is to get that ticket by any means necessary."

The next morning, Whispers called his cousin Troy's house to make sure he wasn't there, and sure enough, he was gone. When we got to Troy's house, Whispers sent Kitten to knock on the door. When she nodded her head to give us the signal that everything was clear to make our move, Whispers and I both kicked the door off the hinges and began to search the whole house.

Thirty minutes later, Kitten screamed out, "I found it! I found it!"

Right then, I decided to kill Kitten and Whispers. I shot Whispers in the back of his head when he wasn't looking, and then I shot Kitten three times in her stomach. When she grabbed her stomach, blood got all over the lottery ticket as she fell to the floor. She moved and moaned for a moment, and then she died.

After taking the bloody ticket from her hand, I left town for six months.

The good thing about this situation is I beat Whispers at his own game; I beat him to the draw. Many people in this world are cruddy as a motherfucker. In most cases, it's the person that's closest to you; a motherfucker you would give the world if they'd only asked.

If Whispers would do some dirty shit like that to a member of his family, imagine what someone in your family would do if they thought it would never get out.

STORY FOUR
THUG DRUG ADDICTION

It was the day before Christmas in 2000. I went to Bass Liquor Store in Mount Rainer, Maryland, and to my surprise, I reunited with a female named Sexy-L. She was admired by plenty, loved by many, and hated by few.

Sexy-L was the offspring of an interracial marriage. Her mother was Cherokee Indian and her father was a black Frenchman. Sexy-L stood about 5’6” and weighed about 145 pounds. Most of her weight was in her perfect, round, juicy, phat, heart-shaped ass. She wore her stringy black hair short, more like Toni Braxton or Anita Baker. Her complexion was olive and her looks were beautiful. Sexy-L was a perfect ten.

Back in the day, she had a helluva reputation at the area's nightclubs and go-go spots. She was best known for her seductive, erotic, rhythmical moves on the dance floor. Every man in the club wanted to freak with Sexy-L because she was also known to make a man's dick so hard that he'd cum in his pants. She was vicious during her days of getting her freak on at this nightclub called the Black Hole on Georgia Avenue in Northwest DC.

When I first met Sexy-L, we were at a nightclub on Blansburg Road NE, called the Metro Club. She asked me if I would let her and her girlfriend get in front of me in line.

I said, "Sure, if you let me palm that phat ass of yours."

"That's rude as a motherfucker," she replied. "What kind of question is that?"

"In this world, you gotta give something to get something."

She looked at me and said, "You're right. So, if you decide that you wanna freak with me in the go-go, you gotta give something to get something. You get the picture?"

During the go-go, maybe about an hour and a half later, I bought Sexy-L about five zombies, and boy was she twisted. Drunk as a motherfucker, Sexy-L let me fuck her in the men's bathroom over the face bowl sink.

Anyway, years had passed and times had changed. The next time I saw her was seven years later when we ran into each other on the south side of Washington, DC. Langston Lane is the projects and it's known for its go-hard, killer-type reputation. I saw Sexy-L buying some crack-cocaine over there one day.

She didn't remember me until I grabbed her by the ass and said, "Do you remember when I fucked you over the sink at the Metro Club back in the day?"

Sexy-L turned and looked at me. "I remember your face, and I remember the occasion, but I can't remember your name."

"Magic Mike," I said.

"Yeah, I remember you. What's going on with you these days?"

"I'm just hanging, trying to keep my head above the water. What are you up to around here In Langston Lane?" I asked.

"What do you think?" she replied.

"Smoking crack?" I said.

She laughed and started walking toward a building I

assumed was a crack house. I started walking with her, and we saw a chalk outline of a dead body on the front porch of the joint, as if someone had been killed there the night before. We continued into the place, which I noticed was an abandoned house. I followed Sexy-L up some dark stairs, and when we got to the top, there was a very large pile of dirt that stood about ten feet high and twelve feet wide. You had to balance yourself as you moved around the pile because you could easily fall backward down the stairs. I followed her to the room where there was no floor, but only wooden beams to walk across to a couch that sat in a corner.

There were two people in the room: a thin white man, and a young black female that looked to be between the ages of fourteen and seventeen. Sexy-L walked across the beam to the couch with them and started smoking the crack she had just bought.

I watched as I waited for Sexy-L to finish. I made sure that she didn't get out of my sight because she still looked damn good to me, regardless of the fact that she smoked crack and ran the street. She had a waist like a wasp and an ass like a horse.

I haven't had any pussy in ages, but I knew if I stuck

around, I probably had a good chance of fucking Sexy-L. All I would need was a boulder of that hard white and I could get a shot of that Red Indian pussy.

It didn't take her long to finish the crack she bought, and for sure, she was feening for more. I told her to roll with me and I would get her some more crack.

We left the abandoned apartment building, as well as the entire south side, and headed northwest. We ended up on 7th and T Street NW, where I stole a nigga's stash as soon as I touched down on the block. I saw this young dude put his stash of crack beside the old Howard Theater. Being the bona fide crack head I was, I made my move on his stash when he started drinking that Remy Martin. You snooze you lose!

I looked at Sexy-L and said, "Let's roll, you dig!"

We walked from 7th and T Street NW to 13th and D Street NE. We stopped over an old childhood friend's house named Johnny Blind, who was a good dude. We called him Johnny Blind because he was blind in one eye.

We went down in the basement of Johnny Blind's grandfather's house, where I began counting the bags of crack I had stolen. I counted 250 half ounces of crack-cocaine. That was enough crack to keep Sexy-L with me for a decade.

I gave Johnny Blind a half an ounce for himself, and then I gave Sexy-L a few fifty-sized boulders to smoke as we chilled. We had the best coke smoking party I've ever witnessed. Then the geeking process began to take place.

Sexy-L's geek was to pull lint balls from your clothes, thinking it was coke. She would look at your clothes, pull a few lint balls off, and taste them until her geek mode started to come down. Johnny Blind's geek was looking you in the face and trying to talk, but only one word would come out. He'd look at you with that glass eye that was about the size of a silver dollar and the real eye that was the size of a nickel, and say, "Hit! Hit!" My geek was just sitting with my arms held up to my head, thinking that someone was about to shoot me. Every time I would hit some crack out of the crack pipe or the ash bowl, I'd cover my head with my arms and yell out, "Don't let 'em kill me!" I'll admit that crack smoking is some crazy shit.

Hours had passed and I wanted some head from Sexy-L. I pulled Johnny Blind to the side and asked if I could have some privacy with Sexy-L.

"Sure, Magic Mike, go ahead and beat her pussy up, boy," he said, giving me a high-five before going upstairs.

That's when I made my move on Sexy-L. I pulled my

dick out and aimed it straight toward her mouth. She started jerking it and looking it over, then she smelled it and made a real horrible-looking facial expression.

She yelled out, “Hell fuckin’ no!”

Then she walked out the back door from Johnny Blind’s basement.

I reached down in my pants with my right hand, rubbed my nuts, and took a good, deep sniff of my hand. The odor was so bad I had to vomit, but I hadn’t had anything to eat, so I had nothing in my stomach to come up.

I called her from the top of my lungs. “Sexy-L, hold up for a minute.”

I ran down the block, catching up with her, and she told me that I offended her because my dick smelled like the back of a garbage truck and it had a crusty, cheesy substance around the uncircumcised skin of the head. I apologized, but I kept it gangster with her. I told her that things hadn’t been going too well for me, and due to my problems, I hadn’t really been myself in regards to me being the man I really was. She understood because she felt the same about her own actions.

Sexy-L smiled, gave me a hug, and said, “Let’s get cleaned up and fuck each other’s brains out. I hope the dirty dick is good!"

I looked at her and replied, "You're about to find out why they call me Magic Mike. The dick is the bomb, but the only way you'll find out is if the pussy is any good."

All the sex talk was making us both horny as two rabbits. After selling a few bags of crack, we found ourselves in a hotel room in Crystal City, Virginia. We lit candles, got comfortable, and enjoyed each other's presence the rest of the night. The strange thing about our night together was we both lost the desire and the interest to have sex; it seemed that we needed more of a friend. I think that was the sign of a real love affair in the making.

The next morning came, and after a good night's sleep, a hit of crack was the focus in our head. The hunger pains were secondary. We were back at it all over again, and pussy was the last thing on my mind.

Sexy-L had been a real close friend. She had been hanging around me every day for the last eight months and I still hadn't fucked her yet. For some reason, the friendship meant more to me than having sex with her, or just maybe the cocaine wouldn't let me get down like that. I really did a good job with keeping myself going when I got the chance to steal a drug dealer's stash of drugs by selling the crack to other crack heads, and at the same token, I didn't have to put my neck on the chopping block as often.

Sexy-L used to warn me all the time about stealing drugs from the drug dealers, but I would never listen. The advice would go in one ear and out the other. I guess that old statement my grandmother used to say was true. "Anything you do once you'll do twice." In my case, that was an understatement. If I got away with something, I took shit to the extreme.

Today was the beginning of another week, and Sexy-L wanted to go see her mother to show her face and let her know she was still alive.

"Magic Mike, I need to go to my mom's house because it's been eight months since I've seen or talked to her. I'm pretty sure she has put a missing report out on me."

"Sexy-L, that's the smartest thing you've said since we've been hanging out. I was wondering when you were going to go home," I said.

"Well, it's the smartest thing I've said other than telling you to stop stealing them drugs from them drug dealers," Sexy-L said, as she playfully pushed me on my arm.

We both went to her mother's house and got cleaned up. No one was home when we got there, but hours later, we heard someone putting a key in the door. The hinges squeaked as it opened.

"That's my mother," Sexy-L said, as she walked swiftly to meet her mother as she came in the front door.

Seeing her mother was like seeing a twin of Sexy-L. She was a beautiful woman; she stood about 5'7" and weighed about 150 pounds. Sexy-L's mother was all Cherokee Indian.

"Miss, they call me Magic Mike. I know we haven't met before, but you are a beautiful woman. I clearly see where Sexy-L gets all her great looks and features from," I said.

"Young man, my name is Mrs. Rhamcheritar, and at this moment, I am so happy to see my daughter. I haven't seen her in a very long time. Any friend of hers is a friend of mine."

Mrs. Rhamcheritar hugged Sexy-L and talked with her for an hour or two before she took her shower and cooked us all something to eat.

"Mike, I'm so glad you brought Lisa home. I want to thank you so much."

I didn't know Sexy-L's first name was Lisa, and I really didn't know she had a nice home with a sweet mother to come home to. I kinda figured there was more to Sexy-L than what presently met the eye.

Mrs. Rhamcheritar cooked lamb chops, mashed potatoes, and string beans for us, and I washed the dishes after we ate. I figured that was the least I could do.

Mrs. Rhamcheritar started asking me questions about my family, and I had to tell the sweet woman a whole bunch of lies because my family had disowned me years ago. They wanted nothing to do with me ever since I set my grandmother up to get robbed and raped by a sex offender that lived across the street from her.

"Where do your parents live? Should I call your family to let them know you're safe?" Mrs. Rhamcheritar asked. "When was the last time you saw your mother?"

Those were the kinds of questions she asked, but deep down inside, it was killing me to even think about it. I told her that my mom was a single parent struggling to raise two kids. I also told her that my father went to the store to get a loaf of bread fifteen years ago and never returned. That was the last time my mother ever saw my father.

Mrs. Rhamcheritar gave me her deepest sympathy in regards to my situation, but I think she knew I was lying and I was nothing more than a hungry, homeless crack head.

******

Sexy-L came downstairs and gave me some pajamas to put on. Then I went upstairs to get settled and watch a little television. Sexy-L and her mother must have had a deep discussion about me, because when I sat at the table with them about an hour later, there was only silence between the three of us.

Mrs. Rhamcheritar said, “Why don’t the two of you stay here for a few days and get some rest?”

I was hoping like hell Sexy-L agreed to stay, because a warm bed, an icebox full of food, and cable TV sure sounded good to me. Sexy-L agreed to stay for a few days so we both could chill out together and get some rest.

“I guess I’ll get myself ready for bed now. Magic Mike, as long as you treat my daughter well and respect her as a female no matter what she does, you will always be welcome in my house, okay?” Mrs. Rhamcheritar said.

“I really appreciate your hospitality. Thank you so much, Mrs. Rhamcheritar,” I said, as she hugged Sexy-L and gave her a kiss on the right side of her jaw.

We sat up for a while playing cards and talking about

our future together. I promised her that I would get my life back in order. After our conversation, we decided to go to bed. I slept in Sexy-L's bed with her. We pulled the warm comforter back, looked each other in the eyes, and smiled. I could tell from the look in her eyes that she had more on her mind than just going to sleep.

"Take those pajamas off," Sexy-L said.

She had on a see-through bodysuit that reminded me of the bodysuit Cat Woman wore in *Batman*. The bodysuit had a hole at the bottom where the pussy could be an easy target.

Sexy-L started licking all around the head of my dick until it got as hard as an iron pipe. Then she turned around and got on all fours so I could bang that pussy like Mike Tyson banging out his opponents in his younger years.

Her pussy was just as I thought it would be, clean-shaven, pink, and fit like a hand in a glove.

"This was well worth the wait," I said softly in her ear.

Sexy-L started breathing harder and harder, while squeezing my body tight and digging her fingernails into the skin of my back. We made love all night, and the good part about it was that my nuts weren't crusty and they definitely didn't smell like shit! I guess that meant I couldn't offend Sexy-

L this time.

The next morning came, and when we realized Mrs. Rhamcheritar had already left for work, we began to have sex all over again. This time it got out of hand and we really got nasty.

Sexy-L pushed everything off the kitchen table, and I started pulling food out of the refrigerator. I poured some Hershey's syrup on her whole body, stuck a banana up her pussy, poured some Smucker's caramel flavored syrup on the banana, and ate the banana out of her pussy. I also put ten purple seedless grapes up Sexy-L's ass and ate each one out with the tip of my tongue. I only wanted to please her in case I left something out last night. You can't be fakin' when it comes to fuckin', pointblank!

That lasted for an hour, or should I say, it lasted until she couldn't cum anymore. Sexy-L started doing some real freaked-out shit back to me, but I wouldn't dare go into detail about that side of her.

Later that evening, I decided that I would go and see what I could get into. I had this overwhelming desire come over me, and it was as if I was helpless in defending myself. Crack-cocaine was calling me. Sexy-L stayed at home while I went on my binge.

"I hope you be careful out there, because you know them people are trying to set you up to hurt you," Sexy-L calmly said.

"I know, but don't worry about that. I'm Magic Mike. I'm too big of a cat to be set up by some kittens, you feel me?" I replied.

"I feel you," she said.

Sexy-L looked me in the eyes and made me promise that I would come back later. I made her a promise so that she wouldn't worry, and then she started kissing me for a very long time, putting her tongue in my mouth almost down my throat.

I grabbed her close to me, with both my hands palming her ass. "I'm part of your world now, and there's no turning back. We are inseparable, baby," I said.

"Are you my man?" Sexy-L asked.

"Yeah, I couldn't wait for you to ask me that question."

"So, this means you're my little crack head boyfriend," Sexy-L said, and we both laughed until our stomachs hurt.

She went back in the house and I went on my mission. I felt so clean and well rested that I wondered why I was out chasing the white ghost all over again.

Before I knew it, I was on 7th and T Street NW back in one of the youngin's stashes again. This time the drugs belonged to a dude name Wicked, who was a hit man for one of the most notorious drug gangs in the history of Washington, DC.

I saw Wicked's car from a distance and also noticed his 500 series Mercedes Benz had a flat tire on the front left side. When I asked Wicked if he wanted me to change the front tire for him, he threw me the keys to his car and said, "Take care of that. I'll pay you when you finish."

I opened the trunk of Wicked's Mercedes Benz to get the tire and the jack, and that's when I saw a black backpack. I fumbled around as if I were looking for the spare tire and looked in the black backpack. To my surprise, I saw five kilograms of pure crystal-white powdered cocaine. I took the backpack and ran as fast as I could down 7th and Florida Avenue NW.

A metro bus was just pulling from a bus stop, and that was my only chance to make a fast move out of that neighborhood. So, I jumped on the back of the bus and held onto the screen that covered the back window. I was scared half to death.

Now the other half that felt no fear was the half that didn't get shot up or the shit beaten out of my ass. I really didn't have anywhere to run or hide because my mother put me out, my grandmother cut me off, and the rest of my family didn't fuck with me. I never had a close friend in my entire life, and now I had the biggest drug gang in Washington, DC out to kill me.

My first thought was to call the police and tell them who was out to kill me in case if they found me dead somewhere, but that meant I would have to tell them why they'd be out to kill me. Not to mention about thirty-eight percent of that gang consisted of metropolitan police officers. So, I couldn't do that.

Instead, I ran to a nearby telephone booth to call Sexy-L, but I forgot that I never asked her for her mother's home telephone number. I also knew I couldn't keep walking around with that backpack full of cocaine on my shoulder. I would definitely get in trouble with the law if I looked to be suspicious or if Wicked caught me with it.

I decided to go to a Safeway store in NE. Once inside, I got one brown paper bag and one plastic Safeway bag. I put the five kilograms of cocaine inside the Safeway bags and threw the backpack in the trash.

I didn't have any money on me, so I made my way to Delaware Avenue SW, where I met some people a while back named Milk Bone and his girlfriend Veda. They were the type who would smoke crack occasionally only if someone came over to get them high.

I sat in the hallway of their apartment building, took about three ounces out of one of the kilos, and then knocked on their door.

I heard a voice say, "Who is it?"

"Magic Mike," I said.

Veda opened the door and gave me a warm hug. "It's been a long time since we've seen you. Where have you been?"

"I've been around doing a little of this and a little of that, if you know what I mean," I said.

I asked Veda to cook up the powdered cocaine for me while I used the bathroom. She took out an empty glass mayonnaise jar and a box of Arm & Hammer and mixed both the cocaine and the Arm & Hammer together. Then she cooked the cocaine until it became a cocaine-based gel. A few minutes later, it dried until it was a rock-like form better known as freebase. I left the kilos in the bathroom because I didn't want to seem as if I was being too protective of the bag.

Suddenly, I started to get paranoid about the bag being out of my sight. Every five minutes, I would run to the bathroom to see if the bag was still there, because in this town, you gotta keep your eyes on your fries.

When I came out of the bathroom, Veda was in the kitchen. I asked her where Milk Bone was, and she informed me that he was locked up and had been incarcerated at Lorton's Occoquan Facilities for about nineteen months.

Quickly, I thought their place would be a great spot for me to lay low; I just had to work my way into the picture. Once the crack had dried rock solid, I started cutting pieces down to smoke with Veda.

Veda knew every crack head in the Delaware Avenue dwelling projects. That made things a lot easier for me to sell a good portion of the crack-cocaine. By the early hours of the morning, I had clocked about $2,800 and was still pumpin' like crazy.

Veda had fallen asleep at about 3:30 A.M. I was tired as hell myself, but I wasn't going to sleep. I was too scared. I must have smoked about a half an ounce of crack to stay awake, and as usual, I got paranoid and started tripping out. What was really freaking me out was Wicked stayed on my conscience.

Veda woke up about 9:00 A.M. and started cooking breakfast. I was sitting in the very same spot when she left for bed.

"Are you hungry?" she asked.

I couldn't say a word because I was geekin' from the last twenty hits I took from the glass crack pipe I was smoking from.

Veda cooked a very big breakfast for us, but I could not eat anything. My nerves were shot, and my paranoia for Wicked had me feeling like a reindeer being stalked by a hungry lion waiting for me to make the wrong move.

I noticed that Veda had gone into the bathroom, and remembered that the five kilos were still in there on the floor. I had no choice but to bust in the bathroom and get the bag before she looked in it to see what it was.

As I forced the door open with my shoulder, I snatched the plastic Safeway bag out of her hands as she began to look at the contents.

"Bitch, what the fuck are you doing?" I screamed out at her.

She stared at me and softly said, "You don't have to curse at me like that."

"I am so sorry for saying that to you. I just have a lot of stuff on my mind. That's all."

I gave her a hug to show my sincerity, but I think she could tell there was something wrong; she just couldn't put her finger on it.

I looked at the clock on the wall and saw that it was approaching twelve noon. It was a long night for me, so I asked Veda to call me a cab. When she asked me for the address, I said, "742 Seventh Street Northwest." That was the address to the poolroom on T Street. I didn't want her to know the address to Sexy-L's mother's house. If she didn't know anything, she couldn't tell anything, especially if anything was to go down as far as Wicked was concerned.

The cab arrived at Veda's house in less than five minutes. All I could remember was getting in the cab and giving the driver a twenty-dollar bill. The next thing I knew, I was fast asleep. I was so tired that it seemed I had just closed my eyes when the cab driver started yelling, "Sir, sir, we are at your destination."

I opened my eyes to find that we were right in front of

the poolroom on 7th and T Street NW. Wicked was sitting in his Mercedes Benz in front of the poolroom, and the cab driver pulled up beside his car. When I saw Wicked, I immediately told the cab driver to pull off.

"Hurry up! Hurry up! Pull off, please!" I said in a frightened tone, while sliding down in the backseat.

The cab driver got mad and started arguing with me about his fare. "I'm not going any further! That's why I don't deal with young people, because they got too much shit with them. Get the fuck out of my cab before I kill your ass, now!"

As I looked out of the corner of my eyes, I saw Wicked and his crew walking toward the cab. When several shots intended for me were fired at the cab, the cab driver pulled off as fast as he could.

I started yelling out to him, "They're trying to rob you, sir! Keep going! Faster! Faster! Drive faster, damn it..."

Wicked pulled beside the cab on Florida and Rhode Island Avenue NW and shot into the cab several times, hitting the driver in the arm and leg. I had ducked.

Without a scratch, I raised my head up to see where we were since the gunfire stopped. The cab driver had taken some shortcuts, some backstreets, and finally he lost Wicked. He was so scared and hurting that he put me out of his cab, saying, "Here, take your motherfuckin' money back. I don't even want it. You could've gotten me killed, you fool!"

I got out of the cab on Capitol Avenue NE in Ivy City and walked to New York Avenue NE. Just as I got to the McDonalds, I heard a horn blow at me. I never looked to see who it was; I just kept walking. The horn blew several more times, so I looked over and it was Mrs. Rhamcheritar. I was so glad to see her that I ran to her 1989 convertible twin turbo Nissan 300ZX and hopped right in the passenger seat.

"I am so glad to see you, Mrs. Rhamcheritar."

She smiled and said, "I'm on my way home. Are you going my way?"

I looked at her and replied, "There's really a God above, because you couldn't have caught me at a better time. You are the angel that watches over me."

Mrs. Rhamcheritar pulled off so fast that you could hear the back tires skidding on the pavement as she moved the clutch to another gear. Mrs. Rhamcheritar asked me what I had been doing all day. I told her that I spent most of the day filling out job applications and looking for any type of job lead.

I could tell she didn't believe me. She stopped at a red

light, took off her sunglasses, and said, “Magic Mike, don’t play with me, boy. Do you smoke crack?”

“Yes and no.”

“Now what does that mean?” she asked.

“That means yes when I can and no when I can’t,” I said.

She laughed as the light turned green. “I want to help my daughter get off that junk. That stuff is killing her, and I can’t sit and watch her die in front of my face.”

I shook my head because I was feeling her on that regardless of me being in the same predicament. At least Sexy-L had a mother that cared; my mother didn’t give a fuck whether I lived or died. Mrs. Rhamcheritar said she wanted to help me, as well, but deep down inside, I didn’t know what the fuck I wanted.

When we got to the house, Sexy-L had hotdogs and baked beans cooked for us, as if she knew I would be there. I hugged Sexy-L and gave her a kiss. She held me so tightly that she squeezed the breath out of me.

“You cooked that food like you knew I’d be here tonight,” I said, while looking at her.

Sexy-L responded by saying, “No, I didn’t know if you

were coming or not, but if you didn't, I would've had a big problem with that. Believe me!"

"I wanted to call you last night, but I didn't know the telephone number."

"Man, fuck you! Where did you stay last night?" she asked coldly.

"I stayed in southwest over my main man Milk Bone's house."

"What were you doing over there where you couldn't come home to me?" she asked.

"I'll tell you what. You come in the bedroom and I'll show you why," I said.

We went in the bedroom, and I showed her the five kilos and the money I made from selling during the early morning hours.

Her eyes got as big as golf balls when she looked in the Safeway bag. "Boy! Where in the hell did you get all of that shit? Oh, my God, help me, please."

"I saw a backpack full of coke in Wicked's trunk, so I just stole it and ran. That's why I didn't come here last night."

Sexy-L looked at me and walked out of the bedroom.

"What's wrong?" I asked, while following behind her.

"They're going to kill you, pointblank, boy," she said, then put her arms around me and wouldn't let go.

I kissed her on the lips and whispered softly in her ear, "I love you very much."

As tears rolled down her face, she pleaded, "Please stop that nonsense, please. I don't want you to get killed."

Sexy-L then went into the kitchen and fixed me a plate. I just sat there, thinking about the situation I had gotten myself into and realizing that I was in more trouble than it really seemed. She was right. When someone's out to kill you, you're in a bad situation - plain and simple.

We both sat at the table in silence. Suddenly, Mrs. Rhamcheritar opened her bedroom door and came out into the kitchen where we were sitting.

"Why are you two sitting there with long faces like someone is getting ready to die or something?"

Sexy-L looked at me and started to cry, then ran in her bedroom.

"What's going on?" Mrs. Rhamcheritar asked.

"I don't know. Maybe she had a bad dream or something," I replied.

We both knocked on Sexy-L's bedroom door, but she

wouldn't open it or say anything. A few hours later, she opened her bedroom door and stood in the doorway sucking her thumb and twisting her hair like she was a little girl.

"I'm sorry, boo. I think I'm in love with you, and I can't picture life without you," Sexy-L said.

"You need to ease up on yourself and don't get worried so much. I'm not going anywhere and nothing is gonna happen to me," I tried to assure her.

Sexy-L wasn't biting on those words, but she acted as if she had faith in me anyway. I'll never forget the look on her face, which spoke the words 'Boy, your life is over!' loud and clear.

Mrs. Rhamcheritar had taken a nap for a few hours during the time Sexy-L locked herself in her bedroom. I told Sexy-L to go talk with her mother and let her know that everything was fine. Sexy-L's mother looked a little worried before she took her nap, and I didn't need two women under the same roof worried and under pressure.

******

A week had gone by, and Sexy-L and I had been smoking crack ever since I stole those kilos. I realized how the things we loved to do could be the very things that could cost us our lives. Although Wicked hadn't caught up with me yet, the cocaine was doing a great number on killing us both, not to mention the mental stress that was killing us slowly.

After smoking coke for the last seven nights, I figured it was time to go out and make some money. I had Sexy-L call a cab for me. Before leaving, I gave her every dime I had in my pocket to split with her mother for providing me with room and board. The last time I had been out in the streets was the night I stayed at Veda's joint. I was a bona fide crack head, and that was a part of my life I didn't want Sexy-L to get to know about me.

Veda's joint was my next move, so I headed to southwest DC to get my hustle on. I took the kilos with me, and the other one I broke down. Before I left, I gave Sexy-L about an ounce to hold her down and keep her lungs out of the street.

During my ride to southwest, I realized I couldn't keep traveling with this amount of cocaine every day. I really needed a spot to hide this shit, bottom line. The first person I thought about was a friend named Lil' Chris, but then I thought that he'd never take me seriously because he knew I was a crack head. A second thought popped in my head. I could hide the cocaine in Sexy-L's mother's house without either one of them knowing where it was. *Yes, yes. That's the move,* I thought to myself. I would explore that option later.

It was about 2:00 P.M., and I was just arriving at Veda's apartment. It was mid-November, but it seemed like it was a hot summer day in July. Veda was in her window, as if she had been expecting me.

"Magic Mike! Hey, baby. I've been waiting for you. Where have you been?" Veda screamed.

Her voice echoed off the walls of the projects like a voice echoing in the mountains. The bitch was as happy as a homosexual with fifty dicks to choose from.

I couldn't get out of the cab before she said, "I got everything you need to cook that shit up."

When I got in Veda's apartment, she had new crack pipes, cooking bowls, and even a brand-new scale. I really didn't know what I was doing as far as matching the quantity of crack to the proper number of weight, so I stuck with selling the dimes, twenties, and fifties. I gave Veda seven grams of crack for letting me use her joint to hustle and do my dirty work out of. She headed to her bedroom, and I didn't hear anything from her until three hours later.

All of a sudden, the sound of gunfire erupted. Pow...pow...pow....bang...bang...bang was all you heard for about three minutes, and then the sound of tires skidding from the scene as people started screaming all over the Delaware Avenue project dwellings. Three little black kids, ages seven, five, and three, were killed instantly as they stood at a Good Humor ice-cream truck. From Veda's window, I could see people standing over the children with looks of fear, but hope on their faces. About ten police cars, two fire trucks, and four ambulances assisted the three children, but it was too late.

Veda dropped the coke, the measuring cup, and the strainer on the floor. She ran as fast as she could out the door to the children because she knew them.

"I used to baby-sit these kids!" Veda screamed aloud as she cried.

Still, the police would not let her beyond the yellow crime scene tape that roped off the area.

The parents of the deceased children arrived on the scene. The three mothers looked to be single parents raising the children without the fathers. Neither police nor bystanders could calm the three women down, especially when two medical examiner trucks pulled up to get the bodies.

Four different news channels were covering the story.

"It is a day of tragedy, misfortune, and heartbreak for these young mothers. A day that will be gone in a few hours, but never forgotten," one reporter said, as he stood in front of a production camera.

Veda came in the apartment crying as she fell into my arms. I tried to calm her down, but her feelings were too involved.

"Veda, you need to relax and calm yourself down. I don't like to see you disorderly like this. There's nothing we can do but support the mothers of those children. If you fall to pieces, who's gonna be strong for the mothers of those children?" I said, while wiping her face with a damp washcloth.

Finally, Veda pulled herself together and went back to cooking the cocaine for me. She talked about Milk Bone as she helped me bag the cocaine up to sell. She asked me to spend the night at her place that night because she was scared, and since Milk Bone was locked up, she was in need of some good lovin'. I told her that I would, but I knew I had to come up with the best excuse I could possibly come up with to leave because for one, I was selling drugs out of her home, and two, I had too much of that crack to stick around and let the police run up on me in her joint.

Hours had passed and everything was back to normal, except for the bloodstains from the children that were still visible on the concrete. Everyone in the neighborhood held candlelight vigils and made a memorial for the children by putting teddy bears, balloons, toys, T-shirts, champagne bottles, liquor bottles, and candy where the three children were murdered.

I started selling my crack as I had intended. Veda went to the liquor store and bought some Remy Martin 1738, a pack of Newport cigarettes, grain alcohol, lighters, and some razor blades. I got my hustle on while we both got high and drunk as a motherfucker. I ended up staying that night. In fact, I stayed several more.

Veda got extremely drunk and started sucking my dick while I was smoking crack that night.

"Does it feel good like this, baby?" Veda asked.

"Hell, yeah, ain't nothing like getting some slow neck while you're smoking crack at the same time."

Veda laughed and continued sucking my dick. She was too cute of a young woman to be a crack head. She had a high yellow complexion, pink lips, and a short afro haircut. Veda was cut up from the butt up.

Nightfall hit and we were still chillin'. I told Veda that I appreciated her letting me clock some cash out her spot and that I respected her for being a true soldier. I kept running on and on with the respect thing, when all of a sudden, she had my dick parked in her mouth all over again like a Cadillac stretch limousine in a carwash. She had the motherfucker so soaked up with spit I thought she used some Tide soap powder or something. Now I see why Milk Bone made her his main woman; she really got the job done. Veda was a true champion at dick eating, and for those bitches out there who want to keep a man, be like Veda.

"I want you, Magic Mike! I want you to be my man. I need your strength and I need your love," Veda said.

That's a bunch of shit, I thought.

Now why would this bitch try to jump me out there like that knowing that Milk Bone and I were cool? He was nothing to play with. I really violated the respect by fucking Veda, which could add more heat to my present situation. I didn't want another motherfucker after me, especially a friend. It was too late for that, though, because I had already put my dick in her head and her ass. So, it would now depend on if he ever found out and/or what he felt for her. Some shit like that could cause a war between him and me; it happens all the time between friends. Personally, when a bitch does what Veda did, you got to let her go, because anything a bitch would do once they would do again and again.

At this point, I knew I had to leave Veda's spot because I might get caught up some kinda way. Plus, the bitch was trying to run con on me now. I didn't like the feeling I was getting inside, so I decided to roll. I got a ride from a crack head to Lil' Bits, another friend of mine who lived in Potomac Gardens in SE.

Lil Bits was one tough bitch, but most of all, she was family. I remember when she was about to get put out of her apartment and child protective services was gonna take her four kids. Lil' Bits went on a serious move by kidnapping a nigga who had all the dope on Georgia Avenue NW.

Lil' Bits pulled up in an all-black 300 Lexus, brand new off the showroom floor, to talk to me on 15th and Independence Avenue SE. I noticed I kept hearing someone yelling and banging on the back of the Lexus. When I asked Lil' Bits if she heard noises coming from her trunk, she got very quiet to listen.

"I know who that is," Lil' Bits said, then opened the trunk.

There lay a man with duct tape over his mouth and around his wrists and legs. Lil' Bits punched him in the face a couple times, then picked a red brick up off the ground and hit him as hard as she could in his forehead with it.

"I told you to stop doing that shit, now didn't I? Next time, I'm going to kill your ass!" Lil' Bits screamed.

She asked me if I needed anything. I was so scared that I wiped my fingerprints off the car and got the fuck away from her. Lil' Bits was the type of female that was down for whatever. If it was going down, it was going down with her.

I stopped at Lil' Bits' place at Potomac Gardens, and as I walked into her building, I saw three young guys selling drugs. I knocked on Lil' Bits' door. While waiting for someone to answer, I heard her children playing on the other side. Lil' Bits opened the door, and to her surprise, it was me.

"Heeeey, what's going on, slim!" Lil' Bits yelled, smiling.

"What's up, shorty?" I said, while hugging her.

I walked into her apartment, and as usual, it was spotless. She told me that she went uptown looking to see me, but people would tell her things like she just missed me or they hadn't seen me. Lil' Bits didn't smoke cocaine; in fact, she didn't get high off anything.

"Are you still on that crack?" Lil' Bits asked.

"Does Gladys Knight know the Pips?" I said.

She laughed and said, "Boy, what am I gonna do with you?"

We sat and talked about old times for hours, and then I dropped the bomb on her, showing her four kilos and the one I had opened.

"Where the hell did you get that from, boy? Did you steal that from somebody? That's a whole lot of shit, slim," Lil' Bits said.

I asked Lil' Bits if she could help me sell the coke. At first, it seemed as if she was a little leery, but she agreed. I gave her nine ounces and told her to give me $7,500 for a quarter of kilo.

She smiled and said, "I'm down wit' that."

I left her place and headed for 13th and D Street NE. As I left Lil' Bits' place, I walked down 11th Street SE and noticed a red 4x4 Blazer sitting on the corner of the block. I paid very close attention to the red Blazer, and as I got closer, I noticed that the windows were all tinted dark black.

"I knew it would only be a matter of time before Wicked caught up with me," I whispered to myself, as I pissed down the right leg of my blue Levis jeans.

I figured it was too late to ask God to bail me out of this one because I got away with so much shit in life anyway.

The red Blazer followed me as I walked down 11th Street SE, then it stopped right in front of me as I stepped off the curb. The passenger's window slowly came down, but only enough so I could see a pair of eyes looking at me.

I heard a deep voice scream, "Get in, motherfucker!" Then I saw a hand with a Mac 11 semi-automatic pistol pointed at me. "I said, get in, motherfucker! Now!" the deep voice screamed out again.

I looked at the dark tinted window with the gun pointed at me and said, "I'm just a crack head, sir. I don't have any money," while showing him my two empty front pockets.

"Bitch motherfucker, don't make me punish your ass, nigga. Get in, bitch!" the deep, scary voice hollered out at me.

I started to run, but I heard a click, as if the Mac 11 was being prepared to be fired.

"Go ahead and run; take this for a joke," the deep voice angrily said.

I slowly walked to the back passenger's side door as someone opened it for me to get into the truck. To my surprise, it was a friend from Elliot Jr. High School named Crazy Frank. We used to play hooky from school and fuck the bitches at his mother's house when she would leave for work.

"I scared the shit out of your ass, didn't I?" he screamed out, laughing.

I didn't find it funny at all due to my present situation, but I was glad it wasn't the real thing. After the joke was over, I asked Crazy Frank to give me a ride to Ivy City. Crazy Frank and I shook hands when he dropped me off, and I headed for Capital Avenue NE to a crack house to sell some of the coke.

I knocked on the door of the crack house and noticed that I heard children crying, but no one answered the door. I stood there for about five minutes before I turned the doorknob and let myself into the apartment. I saw two toddler children, both under two years old, crying on the floor, while three females lay slumped on the couch dead, all with gunshot wounds to the head. Blood was everywhere, and the children were also soaked in blood from climbing onto their mothers. It was a shame to see those children crying with blood all over their faces.

With a few kilos of cocaine in a bag, three dead females, and two kids crying for their dead mothers, I did the next best thing and got the fuck out of dodge. I ran toward Montana Avenue NE and didn't stop running until I got to the Montana Avenue carwash where I caught a cab to Sexy-L's mother's house. When I got in the house, Mrs. Rhamcheritar was sitting at the kitchen table with a disturbing look in her eyes.

"How are you doing, Mrs. Rhamcheritar?" I asked.

"I'm fine, but I haven't seen Lisa in three days," she said sarcastically. "Lisa has been so worried about you that she wouldn't eat or sleep. Where have you been anyway?" she screamed.

I really didn't have a good answer for her, but I did say that I stayed at a friend's house for a few days because a close friend had a death in his family.

I sat up all night waiting for Sexy-L, but she never showed. Now I felt what she felt inside when I was missing for days.

The next morning, Mrs. Rhamcheritar fixed breakfast since it was the weekend and she didn't have to work. We both talked about Sexy-L and me getting our lives together and moving to another city or state.

"I think you and Lisa should get into a drug treatment program and straighten your lives out first, because life is too short to be living a life of hell," Mrs. Rhamcheritar said, as she looked over the top of her reading glasses.

"When Sexy-L comes home, I will talk to her about our present situation and make preparations for a big change," I said.

I gave Mrs. Rhamcheritar five hundred dollars for groceries and little things she might need around the house. When she decided to go to the Giant food store, I took a shower. Suddenly, a thought popped into my mind.

I should look around the house for a spot to hide the kilos of cocaine.

"Yes!" I screamed, while jumping out of the shower.

I looked everywhere in the house and nothing seemed to be a good spot, until I looked behind the refrigerator. I put all of the cocaine in the back of refrigerator on top of the motor. Since every kilo was carefully packaged in plastic and the thick tape that covered it, I figured there wouldn't be any problems. I pushed the refrigerator back in place as if it had never been moved.

Later, Mrs. Rhamcheritar came home from shopping. We put the groceries away and talked for a while. She told me that she took a special liking to me as if I were her own son. That really touched me inside, because all I ever wanted was to feel like I belonged to someone. I never felt or understood the true meaning of family. Now through Mrs. Rhamcheritar and Sexy-L, I believed there was such a definition.

More than two weeks had passed and I thought about Lil' Bits. She was in my debt, so I decided I would give her a call. The telephone rang ten times before someone answered.

"Hello?" a young woman answered.

"May I speak with Lil' Bits?" I asked.

"You have the wrong number," the young woman said.

My heart dropped to my stomach when she said that. I hung the telephone up and redialed the phone number Lil' Bits wrote down on the paper she gave me. The telephone rang again several times only for a little kid to answer and tell me the same thing. The kid told me that the number I dialed was the one I repeated to him, but no one lived there by the name Lil' Bits.

I immediately told Mrs. Rhamcheritar that I needed to go see my mother, but that was a lie just to go look for Lil' Bits.

I caught a cab to Lil' Bits' apartment in Potomac Gardens, and to my surprise, the bitch had moved. Yep! The bitch rolled out on me. I always looked at her as family, but this kinda shit happened to people all the time and this was the shit you had to look out for, especially from the motherfuckers that came from the sandbox with you. When we trust or give our hearts up easily, this is what we get back in return. Love and trust are the very things that one must earn from you and be easily given.

To make things even worse, when I got back to Sexy-L's house, a strong odor lingered through the entire house. Mrs. Rhamcheritar asked me what I thought it could be. I knew what it was off the breakaway, but I had to play it off. I had to act as if I didn't know what was going on or what it could possibly be.

After Mrs. Rhamcheritar went to bed, I moved the refrigerator and looked to see what had happened. I realized that the four and a half kilos had melted because they were too close to the hot motor of the refrigerator. My whole life had just melted away with those kilos. My plans were to go to Wicked and give him back everything, but now this changed the whole plan. I was up shit's creek now. Lil' Bits ran off on me, the rest had melted, and Wicked was looking all over

Washington, DC to kill me.

******

About 3:00 A.M., Sexy-L came home, and the moment I heard her come in the door, I got butterflies in my heart and my stomach because I was so happy she was home. I lay in the bed pretending to be asleep. She jumped on top of me, just as happy to see me as I was in seeing her.

"Boy, I see you peeping outta both of your eyes," Sexy-L said.

We held each other tight as we kissed. Afterwards, Sexy-L went to take a shower and get fresh so we could have sex. When she got out of the shower, I must have made her cum about seven or eight times before I did.

The next morning, Sexy-L told me she had been out for nearly a week looking for me, and through her travels, she saw Wicked and his crew. She said he didn't say anything to her, but he gave her a suspicious look of retaliation. I told Sexy-L what had happened to the kilos of cocaine and she got so scared and disappointed that I believed if we were near a bridge, she would've pushed me right off.

"What on earth made you put that shit in the back of my mother's refrigerator? I don't know what the hell you were thinking about when you did that stupid-ass shit!" Sexy-L yelled.

"I thought it was the best place to hide it in case the police came here," I said.

"The shit shouldn't be at my mother's house in the first place, Magic Mike!"

I looked at Sexy-L and shook my head. It didn't matter when we were smoking the shit in there, so what was the problem now? I guess 'cause the shit melted, that was the problem.

"Sexy-L, I know things have been a little off-track between us due to our addictions, but I want us to get our lives together and get away from all the negative bullshit that surrounds us," I said, while hugging her.

Sexy-L looked at me, rolled her eyes, moved my arm from around her, and walked out the door. I stood there in my boxer shorts with a towel around my neck as she slammed the front door in anger. I put my clothes on and tried to catch her, but it was too late; she had already jumped on a bus heading to the south side.

I caught up with her hours later in the Langston Lane apartments. She must have been smoking crack from the time she left home to the time I caught up with her because she was definitely in her geek mode. Sexy-L called me the moment she saw me on the block. She pulled out about seven grams of crack and a glass stem, and we smoked for about an hour and a half at someone's house. When the entire seven grams of crack was gone, this big black motherfucker named Lee Tucker asked Sexy-L if he could make her a proposition.

She looked at me and asked, "Can I go make us this easy, quick money?"

"Sure, why not?" I said, as I peeked around the house.

Sexy-L went into another room with Lee Tucker. Things were quiet at first, and then all you could hear was Sexy-L screaming out at the top of her lungs for dear life.

"Ouch...stop! Please...oh, my God! My stomach hurts! That dick is too big. Magic Mike, help!"

I peeked through the door, and all I could see was a big black man that stood about 6'5" and 270 pounds, with a dick about sixteen and a half inches long digging in and out of Sexy-L's pussy. At that point, I didn't see anything easy or quick about the money she was making. I knew one thing; with a dude that big and tall, with a dick three times bigger than mine, Sexy-L was on her own. I wasn't coming between that.

Besides, that's what a pussy was made for. The dick was built for a man, but made for a woman.

Lee Tucker fucked Sexy-L for two long hours, while she cried out in pain the whole time. Suddenly, things got quiet. Lee Tucker walked out of the bedroom door, leaving Sexy-L lying in the bloody bed half-awake with blood flowing from her pussy.

She feebly said, "I need to go to the hospital," and asked me to call an ambulance for her because the pain was unbearable.

Lee Tucker had busted her pussy wide the fuck open, causing much pain and injury to her insides. Sexy-L stayed in the hospital for about four weeks getting operations and having all kinds of tests ran on her body. I went to see Sexy-L every day up at Howard University Hospital. They recommended that she stay in an inpatient drug treatment program for six months.

I got word that Wicked and his crew was looking all over the city for me. I got so scared that I checked in the drug treatment program with Sexy-L for six months to save my life for at least the length of the program. It was like starting life all over again. I was with Sexy-L and we both were alcohol and drug free. My only worry was Wicked and his crew.

The first day in the program, I felt very comfortable, and my inner thoughts told me that was the place I needed to be. There was a roomful of drug addicts and alcoholics that realized they were powerless to their addictions. The drug counselor, Billy, started our first meeting by sharing with us his experiences with his drug addiction. He told us that he could remember a time when he would buy a bag of heroin and his bowels would break the moment the heroin would touch the palm of his hand.

Billy told us that he bought a bag of heroin one day and went in the oil joint where heroin addicts shoot drugs in their arms, but the water was cut off. He said that he went in the bathroom to shoot his dope and the only water in the house to use was the water out of the toilet. When he lifted the toilet seat up, he saw a bunch of shit in the water. Billy said he knew he had to get the heroin in his veins, so he moved the shit to the side with his hand and put enough water In a Wild Irish Rose wine top to use to shoot the heroin.

Another guy named Danny told us one of his stories.

"My name is Danny and I'm a recovering addict," he started. "I can remember one night I was out to get high off my favorite drug of choice, crack-cocaine. That shit ain't no joke. I met a homosexual one night when I was on one of my crack binges. The homosexual had me right where he wanted me when he found out I didn't have any money and he had access to a major bankroll. The homosexual bought enough crack to ask me to suck his dick and fuck me up my ass. With that, I'm gonna keep comin' back," Danny said.

I couldn't help but to laugh at these motherfuckers, because Magic Mike wasn't going out like that and I never knew people would do the things they'd do to get drugs. A few people said they sucked a dog's dick for a piece of crack. Now that was plain ridiculous! Everyone told their story and everyone had some crazy shit to say about their experiences.

Sexy-L and I had found a fuck spot in the program where we could fuck at least three times a day, four times a week. After all the fucking, four months later, Sexy-L wasn't feeling right. The doctor told her that she was twelve weeks pregnant. When Sexy-L told me the news, I was overwhelmed with happiness.

"I'm pregnant with your baby and I want to marry you, Magic Mike. I want us to become a family and make this relationship work between us. Just you, me, and our baby,"

Sexy-L said.

I told her that I felt so good inside about us being a family, and I reassured her that love and security would be the constraints of our relationship.

"I got your back," I said.

"Don't make any promises you can't keep because I ain't going for it," Sexy-L said in a very serious voice.

"Everything is a done deal with you," I said, while looking her straight in the eyes.

I kissed her on the forehead and she kissed me on mine.

"Are you my crack head little boyfriend?" Sexy-L asked, as she laughed.

"Yeah, I'm your crack head little boyfriend," I said, as I laughed with her.

******

Months had passed, we were out of the program, and the baby was due. Sexy-L and I went to Pentagon City Mall to get some things for the baby. I walked to Sexy-L's mother's twin turbo 300ZX and Sexy-L wobbled behind me, holding her pregnant stomach.

As I opened the trunk of the 300ZX, three men with

black hoods over their faces ran up to the car with guns. I took off running, leaving Sexy-L behind, repeatedly hearing the sound of gunfire. I heard at least thirty gunshots.

They shot Sexy-L in the head, stomach, back, and legs. About eight bullets went through the baby and out Sexy-L's back. Wicked and his crew had killed Sexy-L and the baby.

The police came to Sexy-L's mother's house and took me down to the homicide division at police headquarters to ask me questions about what happened, but I didn't tell them anything.

A week later, Mrs. Rhamcheritar held the wake and funeral services for Sexy-L and the baby, which was a girl. Sexy-L wore a pink dress with white lace around the neck and sleeves; the baby wore a white dress with pink lace around the neck and sleeves. Sexy-L was laid to rest with the baby held tight in her right arm.

I know both Sexy-L and the baby paid the ultimate price for something I did, and I'm truly sorry for that. I know they're in a better place and someday I'll see them again.

Put yourself in my shoes. What would you have done?

STORY FIVE
THUG GLITTER AIN'T GOLD

I used to be amazed by the glamorous life of the dope dealers, the pimps, the true players, and the bona fide hustlers. Never did I ever imagine that there were two sides to the game until I ran across a few people who lived it.

Earning the nickname Lucky from my grandfather when I was a child – because at the time my mother gave birth to me, the umbilical cord was wrapped around my neck and the doctor said I was lucky to live the total nine months under those conditions – my grandfather considered me to be a blessing from God. When I got up in age, I moved around the city. I got to know many people in my travels from one side of town to the other. I was always meeting people in one fashion or another.

One humid July summer night in 2001, I met this female named Terri. We exchanged telephone numbers and decided to get together real soon. She was a true to the code ho; that's all she knew and that's all she wanted to be.

I finally called Terri a week later on a Saturday night to see what her plans were for the evening.

"I'm going on the track, or the ho strip if you don't understand the lingo. If you would like to catch up with me, that's where I'll be. The ho strip is New York Avenue Northeast, a block away from the Skylark Lounge," Terri said.

Terri had a large clientele when it came to selling pussy. She had a number of doctors, lawyers, police officers, firefighters, lesbian women, and many others. Terri was twenty-one years old, of African-American descent, and was built like the porno star Diana Devoe that got her brains fucked out in the porno flick *Sugar Walls 14*. She stood about 5'4" and weighed about 125 pounds. She had the prettiest body a man could ever imagine in his bed. Her hair was cut short like an Afro bush, and her complexion was a dark chocolate.

I established a good relationship with Terri because we

hooked up on a daily basis for six months after we met. We ate together, slept together, ran con together, hustled together; we did everything together. Terri always told me that she wanted me to be her pimp, but I didn't have a clue as to what my role would be as a pimp to her since we got so close. I couldn't picture me slappin' her in the face or beatin' her down because she didn't have the money right or make the quota I sent her out to make. Most of the time, I would go on the track with her to watch her back and to keep other men from robbing or raping her. In other words, I was her protection.

I remember going to the Skylark Lounge with her one night. The Skylark Lounge is one of the biggest strip clubs in the Washington, DC area, and it's known for having the best-looking dancers in DC. Terri and I sat at a table and ordered some drinks, when some guy walked up to our table and asked to speak with her. They both walked outside the club, and when Terri came back in, she told me that she was going to suck the guy's dick in his car for seventy-five dollars.

"That's cool. Go do your thing," I said.

Fifteen minutes later, Terri came back in the lounge and handed me the whole seventy-five dollars.

"Everything went fine and we got a lot more money to

make," Terri said, as she sat at the table.

I can do this, I thought to myself. *I can get paid and let her do her thing while I just chill.*

I was starting to feel like the Godfather inside. I had just realized that when a woman hands you some money that she fucked or sucked a dick for, you're the nigga with the juice.

Two hours had passed and we decided to leave the Skylark Lounge. Terri came up with an idea to start recruiting new hoes for our stable. Her plan was to put a young ho on each and every corner of New York Avenue, from the Budget Inn Motel to the Days Inn Hotel at the corner of New York Avenue and Bladensburg Road NE.

"It's time we step our game up. I'm going to pull some of these young hoes up and put them on our team. It's time to make some real money around this motherfucker," Terri said, as she looked around the strip, smoking a cigarette.

"If we put the right efforts in this and use the right strategy, the world could be ours for the taking," I added.

"Lucky, I'm the type of female that goes for the gold! I'm the motherfucker that put a jackass in the Kentucky Derby and damn near won. I try my hand at any cost," Terri said.

About a month later, everything went as planned. Terri

met five females that were down for anything she asked of them; they were just what she had been looking for. Each one of them had beautiful bodies and a big booty to go with it; they had all the qualities we needed. We had big plans, and I held the feelings of big pimpin' closed tight in the palms of my hands.

We all went to a hotel that Terri and the girls normally rented to sell pussy and transact their business. This particular night was different, though, because we were out to celebrate, have fun, and fuck amongst the seven of us. We smoked weed and got drunk off alcohol. They sucked my dick, and I ate a whole lot of pussy that night. I had to put my employees to the test by fucking everyone to see just what my customers were getting for their money.

Before we engaged in our sexual pleasures, Terri wrote six nicknames down on six small sheets of paper, and each one of the girls had to pick one of the sheets of paper with a nickname on it from the hat.

"From this day forward, the nickname you ladies pick from the hat will be the name you'll be called," Terri said seductively.

Angela picked first. Her nickname became Honey.

Shawanna became Fire, and then Regina picked Blaze. Joan became Seduction, Mattie was Cream, and Terri chose the nickname Queen Bee.

"Everybody strip down butt naked!" Terri yelled aloud.

We took off all our clothes down to our birthday suits. My dick is thirteen inches long and about five inches thick, and it was hard as a motherfucker looking at all those pussies walking around the room.

I started with Honey first. Her name said it all, and the taste of her was as sweet as the honey from the honeycomb. She started giving me oral sex, but my dick was too long and too wide for her small mouth. I looked up and there I saw Fire with two ice cubes in her mouth coming toward the bed. I put my hand out to her as she took Honey's place. Fire went up and down my genital area from the crack of my ass to the top of my dick's head, and the cold temperature made me as stiff as the monument. Blaze and Honey started sucking on my toes since they both felt that my dick was too big for their mouths. Fire continued pleasing me orally, while Queen Bee and Seduction fucked each other in the corner of the room.

The sex party lasted for hours, as the moaning and groaning only got louder. Finally, I hooked up with Queen Bee.

I started slowly with a kiss on her neck. I used my tongue to lick her warm body as she lay in the center of the bed.

"Lucky, I'll never leave you. I'll always be loyal and honest to our commitment as friends, lovers, and partners," Queen Bee said, as I continued to suck her pussy dry.

I acted as if I didn't hear the words she cried out to me, because it was easy to say things, but living up to what a person said was totally different. Time tells you everything you need to know about people. I was the show-and-tell type of person. I believed that a person should make their actions speak louder than the words they said out of their mouth.

Inside the room, everyone had someone in a sexual way, checking out the skills and experience of his or her fellow teammate. All you heard was screams of passion, as the vibrations of an orgasm followed in an order of sequence.

Before we finished the fuck-fest, I summed it up by fucking each of the girls in a doggy-style position, starting with Blaze and ending with Seduction. Since everyone got his or her nut off, it was now time to plan our money mission.

Queen Bee yelled, "The only person who has control as to where and when we go is me!"

Queen Bee made sure the plans went as directed and

the girls followed her suit.

We all headed for the big apple, New York City. None of us knew much about the big city of dreams, but it was well worth a try. We started on Broadway and ended up in Queens. For us, prostitution didn't pay well, but I had a feeling that ignorance to the city was our biggest holdback. We knew a lot went on in New York City, but we didn't know where. In seven days, the girls only made about five hundred dollars among the six of them and that wasn't a good profit. Any professional pimp knows one girl should be able to bring in a thousand dollars on a bad night if your stable of hookers is in the right place.

I decided that we would leave New York and try a couple truck stops near Philadelphia, then hit Las Vegas where they say prostitution is legal. Once we arrived in Las Vegas, I told the girls that was probably where our new home would be.

"This is the city that never sleeps. Let's take a walk through the casinos and look things over before we start layin' our lick down," Queen Bee said.

Queen Bee came up with the idea to have cards made so that our clients could contact us at any time for any occasion. That played a very big part in our business, because the money started rolling in like bets on a casino crap table. The girls turned a few tricks and bought new clothes to go on their dates. Things started to change at that point, so I just laid back and let them do their thing. I went up to the hotel room and got the chance to catch up on some rest and relaxation, as the girls made big moves.

The next day, Queen Bee and the girls decided to rest as well, because they must have fucked about eighty men between the six of them.

About 1:30 A.M., the girls and I went over to the MGM Hotel to line up a couple of dates and pass out our business cards. Queen Bee quickly got a date with two white men that looked to be senators or congressmen. I reflected back to my mind's eye and remembered that I had seen both of those men on the evening news before, but I just couldn't remember their names.

Seconds later, Blaze, Honey, Fire, Seduction, and Cream were picked up by a group of rap stars to fuck, suck, lick ass, and have fun. I couldn't believe my eyes when I saw those guys because they really were big in the industry with some major loot. I told each of the girls to keep it all business and charge five hundred dollars apiece for their services.

About an hour and a half later, I caught up with Queen Bee, and we decided to do some shopping because she had stolen both of the wallets of the men she was dating.

"Baby, I want to buy you some top-of-the-line gear to wear because it's your turn to shine. I got fifteen hundred dollars cash out of them jerks and their credit cards; I'm a bad bitch!" Queen Bee said, as she held her hand out for me to give her a high-five.

Queen Bee really believed in her heart that she could make this line of business work, and she also believed that she could turn this illegal shit into something really positive. I felt her on that, because the thought was the cause of it all. Everybody should have a dream, and selling pussy to get on top was hers.

After a few drinks and a little bit of gambling, Queen Bee and I caught up with the girls.

"Lucky, I think we should all have cell phones to contact each other. What do you think?" Queen Bee asked.

"I think that's a good idea. Then we can always know where everyone is and make sure no bullshit goes down," I said.

"We got one thousand dollars apiece out of them niggas!" Blaze screamed, as the girls showed Queen Bee and me their big bankrolls of money.

"We really got paid this time!" Seduction yelled out.

The girls were so happy they made so much money that they started jumping around and hugging each other. Fire and the rest of the girls held the bankrolls of money in the air.

"Cheers to the good life and to those who contribute to us all getting paid," Queen Bee said, as she collected all of the money from the girls.

She was pimp to all the girls, and my job was to learn how to be a pimp.

"Lucky, this is supposed to be your job for real. You're supposed to collect the money and make sure we're out there making that money for you. You really need to learn the game," Queen Bee said, as she pulled me to the side.

"I think we need to set Lucky up with some real rich bitches to get paid for that good dick he has. What do you think, girls?" Honey said, as I stood to the side with Queen Bee.

Everyone started laughing.

I thought it was kinda funny myself, and it wasn't a bad idea. For the right price, I would fuck Grandma Dynamite.

I left the girls for a while and took a walk through the casino to see what I could see. That's when I ran into a guy named Silky Slim from St. Louis, Missouri. Silky Slim said he was a pimp from the dirty south and that he got big money in the pimp game. I had so many questions to ask him because I was new in the game and eager to learn everything about it. Silky Slim and I clicked right off the top. I liked his style and he liked the enthusiastic interest I held at heart. I felt that I could learn a lot of things from a man in the game like him.

He talked to me for hours about the things I should and shouldn't have to worry about in the pimp game if I didn't start slipping.

"Lucky, this is only the beginning, and many things will become very clear to you about bitches down the line," Silky Slim said. "You must always remember that every ho is different and you must treat them differently. No two hoes can be treated the same. You must keep your foot on their neck and apply pressure as needed, and when that money slows up, somebody needs a major ass whoopin' because some bullshit is in the air somewhere."

After talking to Silky Slim, I felt very confident. I felt so confident that I was ready to try some of that shit on the girls.

When I went upstairs to the room to take a shower, I saw that Queen Bee had left a note that read: *The girls and I went shopping for you. We will buy clothes and shoes for your precious body to wear. Stay sweet and lovable until we see you soon. Love, Queen Bee.*

The telephone rang about three times, and when I picked it up, it was Queen Bee.

"Hey there, my favorite Don Juan. The Queen Bee is a little horny and needs to be stung. What's up with that?" Queen Bee said in a sexy tone.

"Sure, come on up and let the ol' boy put the stinger in the Queen Bee until I paralyze your sexual needs into submission," I replied.

Queen Bee came up to the room, and we made love as we never did before. We got so sweaty during our lovemaking that the girls came upstairs and wiped us down with two big beach towels. After we finished having sex, the girls started clapping and thanking us for such a show. We laughed, but we put in some serious work.

I called Silky Slim's room and invited him to our room so the girls could meet him. I spoke very highly of him because I found his teachings to be stable and promising. The girls didn't like him at first, but I convinced them that he was a good dude.

I asked Silky Slim to show me the ho strip, so we rented a car and took a ride through the Las Vegas town. Silky Slim advised me not to put the girls on the strip because either other pimps would try to take them from Queen Bee or they would hook up with other prostitutes and pick up bad habits.

For months, the plan worked with the girls, but somehow, Silky Slim started stabbing me in the back. I couldn't put my finger on it and I couldn't understand how the friendship between Queen Bee and Silky Slim got closer and closer by the days, but I knew I had to watch all moves. I pulled up on Queen Bee and told her that I didn't like how she had been carrying shit with that nigga. I had to let her know that we came out here as a team and the girls counted on us for leadership.

"Nothing is going on between Silky Slim and me. You and I will always be a team, baby. I just find Silky Slim to be funny and intelligent. He knows a lot about the pimp game and I'm curious. You need to hang around him," Queen Bee said, as she walked away.

"That's bullshit! I don't like the shit that nigga is trying to pull at all," I responded.

"Then you need to take that up with him! You are the man in this situation, right?" Queen Bee said with a smile.

Somehow, I began to feel that Silky Slim was slowly working his way in between the girls and me, separating everything we stood for and everything we dreamed of.

A couple weeks later, Silky Slim said that we should leave Las Vegas and go to his hometown of St. Louis, Missouri. I told Queen Bee that I thought it was a good idea to try another place, but not St. Louis. Queen Bee said she had never been to the dirty south, and she wanted to see what it was like and what it had to offer her. So, we packed our bags and headed for St. Louis, Missouri.

Silky Slim and I had a long talk on the airplane; he reassured me that everything would go well and to understand that I would make big money in the pimp game in St. Louis.

We continued to go over the pimp commandments, the do's and don'ts. Seduction started getting on my nerves by trying to talk to me while Silky Slim was trying to explain the game to me at the same time.

"Bitch! Do you see this man talking to me? What the fuck is so important at this moment that you can't wait until I'm finished talking?" I asked, while gritting my teeth together.

"Lucky, I'm so sorry. I just wanted to tell you that I'm so glad that I met you and Queen Bee. I really look at you and her as my lifesavers," Seduction said to me.

Silky Slim turned to me and stated, "That's how you're supposed to have a bitch feeling about you."

I really didn't know how to respond to what Seduction said to me, so I winked my eye at her and simply said, "You mean so much to me and Queen Bee. More than you could ever imagine."

Queen Bee looked at me with a half-smile and blew a kiss at me.

We arrived in St. Louis at 7:45 P.M., and everyone was ready to eat, rest, and start the next morning off fresh. We ate at a restaurant that served curry foods. It was a laid back, cozy-type of atmosphere that was just right for the girls and me.

After we finished eating, we caught a cab. Silky Slim showed us an inexpensive motel in the city where we could get some rest and the girls could turn a few tricks at the same time.

The money they each made was no comparison to what they were making in Las Vegas, so I started pushing the girls harder to make that money. I started raising pure hell and whooping their asses about that short money.

One thing Silky Slim was right about, I had to start running my stable with a tight fist and then things would fall into place. I remember Silky Slim saying that you must put some major fear in them bitches. If you tell 'em that you would kill 'em, you had better bring them as close to death as you could to keep them bitches scared to death of you.

I called a meeting with the girls about what needed to be done and some issues that needed to be addressed. Most of the girls were fine with the program, but Honey and Fire had a problem with the unity. They felt that the unity was crumbling. I looked at Queen Bee to see what her input would be.

"Those who feel that the unity is crumbling have a good point. Things are coming at us so fast that we are just concentrating on what we came for and not each other, which isn't bad either because everyone has to do their job like we planned. What do you think about that, Lucky?" Queen Bee asked.

"I feel kinda insecure about the loyalty and the unity, also, but Queen Bee is right! We shouldn't get so paranoid. We still have to get what we came for. That loot!" I said to the girls with confidence in my voice.

With Silky Slim gone, I told the girls that we could not let someone we didn't know come between us because he was not in our plans in the first place.

Suddenly someone knocked hard at the room door. I opened it, and it was Silky Slim and two other guys who seemed to be pimps, as well. Silky Slim introduced them to us as Gangster Joe and Pretty Toni. The girls and I also introduced ourselves, but I didn't like the shit this nigga was trying to pull on us. So, I spoke to Silky Slim about it.

"Silky Slim, why would you bring someone to our motel room we don't know or care to meet?" I asked.

"There's no need to get upset, Lucky. These are my friends and I wanted them to meet you and the girls. Is anything wrong with that? I told them that I met you all in the city of sin, and I wanted to hook y'all up with a good connection. We can be a team," Silky Slim said.

"I have my team and it consists of those six girls over there. We don't need any more teammates; our roster is full," I replied with much anger.

Silky Slim, Pretty Toni, and Gangster Joe looked me in the eyes with pure hostility; they had animosity written all over their faces.

Pretty Toni showed no respect to how I felt about the situation at hand. He started telling the girls how beautiful they all looked and how they could break every man on Wall Street. Pretty Toni then grabbed Queen Bee and positioned her body in front of his, where her ass was on his private parts. He started feeling all over her body and running his fingers through her hair as if he had no respect for me whatsoever.

Gangster Joe never said one word. He just watched with a look of death on his face like he'd kill a motherfucker in a heartbeat. I must admit, I was scared as a bitch and didn't know how to deal with the situation, so I just went along to get along.

About an hour later, Pretty Toni, Gangster Joe, and Silky Slim left. I observed them very closely during their visit and discovered that Pretty Toni had some major shit up his sleeve. When I asked Queen Bee what she thought about Pretty Toni and his crew, she told me that she felt very comfortable with all of them. In fact, she thought Pretty Toni was a nice person who knew the pimp game very well. She said she'd like me to loosen up some and learn the game from him. She also mentioned that she felt very comfortable with Gangster Joe because he looked like a good protector, and that was something she had been looking for.

"What do you mean by that?" I asked.

"Lucky, my father was never there to protect me from my fears or people who posed a threat of harm to me. I believe that whatever a woman does in life or whomever she's with, she should always know what position she's in. If a person is in a position and doesn't know where they stand, they are in a bad position. I feel comfortable with all three of them," Queen Bee said with a smile I had never seen on her face before.

When Queen Bee said that shit, I knew I was in a bad position, because I was in a city in the south where I didn't know a damn soul. Furthermore, I got the feeling that Queen Bee was about to flip the script on me. I guess that's how people get when the ball is in their court.

Two days later, Pretty Toni and his crew came back to our motel room.

"Queen Bee, why don't you and the girls come take a ride with me?" Pretty Toni asked.

"Sure, just let me put on my fishnet stockings and my high heels," Queen Bee replied, as she dressed her half-naked body.

Queen Bee and the girls left with Pretty Toni and his

crew on a Thursday evening and did not return until Sunday about one o'clock in the afternoon. I was looking for an explanation when they got back, but no one had anything to say. Therefore, I took it upon myself to ask questions in reference to their whereabouts and actions during those days they were gone.

"You don't ask any questions about nothing! I'm running this program. We stayed at Pretty Toni's house!" Queen Bee screamed.

I punched that bitch right in her mouth and continued to beat the dog shit out of her until I damn near killed her ass. Queen Bee was unconscious when I finally stopped beating her and blood was all over the motel room. The girls started screaming and calling out for help.

When I looked up, I saw Blaze making a telephone call. I didn't know who she was calling, but later I found out that it was Pretty Toni, Silky Slim, and Gangster Joe. When Pretty Toni arrived, there was nothing said between us, but from the look in his eyes, I felt this wouldn't be the last of the situation.

Queen Bee was taken to the hospital by ambulance and admitted due to the bruising of her brain. The girls all moved to Pretty Toni's place, and I had no money or food to eat. I was left in a fucked-up situation and out of the picture.

Fourteen days later, I went to see Queen Bee at the hospital. I walked in her room and saw her in a coma with tubes hooked up to her body. I felt so bad about what I had done to her, but it was too late. My biggest worry was her dying. Between the girls and Pretty Toni knowing I did that shit, I was sure I would be looking at a twenty-five or thirty year sentence.

I decided I'd leave and come back another time. So, I left the hospital, and during my walk, I picked a McDonald's cup up off the ground and held it up as people walked past, begging them for spare change.

I hadn't eaten for a week, and I drank so much alcohol that I started vomiting blood. I lived the life of a bum on the streets for a few weeks because I had no money. I ate out of trashcans, I smelled like shit, and I had to leave the motel room. Pretty Toni kept the girls away from me, so I didn't know the first place to look for them. I was fucked up!

I called the hospital three weeks later and the nurse told me that Queen Bee was out of the coma and doing much better. I walked to the hospital to see her. When I walked in her room, she was sitting up eating her lunch in bed.

"Queen Bee!" I yelled with excitement.

She still had bruises all over her face, but I was so glad that she was getting better.

"I apologize for talking to you the way I did and doing the things I did behind your back. I'm just confused and I'll need some time away from you. I am so scared of you now. You're not who you used to be, Lucky," Queen Bee said quietly.

"That's cool. I'm just glad that you're okay now," I said, as I handed her a red rose that I had picked from someone's yard along the way to the hospital.

Ten minutes later, a delivery company delivered 25 dozen red, white, and yellow roses to her room, along with 200 get-well balloons and 150 get-well cards. I stood there in disbelief. I didn't have a clue as to what happened or what just went down. All I knew was Pretty Toni had manipulated Queen Bee, the girls, and me through Silky Slim. I told Queen Bee how I was living and what had been going on with me, so she gave me five hundred dollars and told me to get a hotel room. I kissed her on the cheek and told her that I would see her in a couple of days. I stepped off at that point.

A week later, I called Queen Bee at the hospital. She told me that she was being discharged and that Pretty Toni and

Gangster Joe were on their way to pick her up. I told her the name and the address of the hotel I was staying in.

A day later, she showed up at my room door. I opened the door to find Queen Bee standing right before my very eyes.

"I thought you would never come see me, but I was wrong, huh? Do you still love me, Queen Bee?" I asked.

"Yes, I will always love you, Lucky. You changed up on me by whooping my ass. Do you know you could've killed me? My mother always said that if you let a man hit you once, he'll do it again, and if you keep lettin' him beat on you, you're putting his life before yours. I'll sell pussy for a nigga, but I ain't having a man beatin' my ass," Queen Bee replied.

I had to respect what she said because for one thing, I loved her. Also, I wanted to be back with the plan. In addition, I had to understand that I was playing a pimp role and had to remember what I came here for; therefore, I had to roll with the punches. To a certain degree, I realized that I had lost Queen Bee to Pretty Toni. Pimps lose prostitutes to other pimps every day in the game. I just needed to learn how to keep a tight game with my hoes and keep in mind that every experience was a learning experience.

Queen Bee and I spent most of the day together. We

made love and had crazy sex all motherfuckin' day. My dick was sore from the dryness of her pussy due to the multiple orgasms. Her pussy got dry as hell. I personally thought that Queen Bee decided to fuck me because she had a guilty conscious, plain and simple.

When people do things behind your back and they know it was some dirty shit they did, they try to do something to compensate for the shit they did to you so they won't have that guilt on their mind when they have to face you. I didn't trip about the shit; I just played it like a true DC nigga.

"Lucky, I plan on coming back to you. I hope you can understand what I'm going through right now. Things are coming at me so fast that I'm not thinking clearly," Queen Bee said, as she held me tight in her arms.

"I guess it's three the hard way, huh?" I said.

"What do you mean by that?" Queen Bee asked.

"I'm talking about Pretty Toni, Gangster Joe, and Silky Slim," I replied, as we both laughed.

Queen Bee went into the bathroom, and after starting the shower, she called for me to join her as she began washing her hair.

"Lucky, come and get in the shower with me!" she

yelled.

"I'm coming right now," I said, while walking to the bathroom.

I got in the shower and we started washing each other's body with the soapy washcloths. I looked in her eyes and gave her a soft kiss on the lips, as I felt her heart race like a racecar in the Indianapolis 500.

"I will always love and respect you no matter what, and whatever happens between us, remember that no one can be as special to me as you," Queen Bee said, as she kissed my lips.

After we took our shower, Queen Bee wanted me to ride with her to Pretty Toni's place. So, we caught a cab and got there about 7:56 P.M. The girls were gone, but Pretty Toni was there alone.

The thing that really puzzled me was everything in Pretty Toni's place was pink. There was a pink couch, pink curtains, a pink eating table, a pink comforter on the bed, and the walls were all painted pink. As I continued looking around Pretty Toni's apartment, I couldn't help but to notice that there was an outrageous number of sexual toys lying around. Leather whips and chains, butt plugs, big and small dildos, peanut butter asshole packing cream, tropical flavored asshole and pussy licking cream, and an assorted box of Clit O Mints.

Pretty Toni was surprised that I showed up with Queen Bee.

"Lucky, I been thinking about you lately. What's been going on with you? I hear you aren't doing so well," Pretty Toni said, as we gave each other a handshake.

I looked at Pretty Toni with a long stare before answering. "With all my girls on your team, how can I afford to eat or live? Yeah, I'm fucked up in the game," I replied, while pulling lint balls out of each of my front pants pockets.

Pretty Toni laughed. "This is a player's world, Lucky. This is a player's world," he said.

As I stood in the kitchen doorway of Pretty Toni's apartment, my mind started to wander. I began to think about the things I was seeing in this man's apartment and the things about him in general. For example, everything in his apartment was pink, so why did he call himself Pretty Toni and why did he spell his name the way he did?

There's something about him I just can't put my finger on, I thought to myself.

Queen Bee steamed three large lobster tails with a couple pounds of shrimp. Pretty Toni opened a bottle of Grey

Goose vodka and poured Queen Bee and me a few drinks as we waited to eat.

"The lobster will be ready in twenty minutes," Queen Bee said, as she put a half cup of beer and raw shrimp in a saucepan.

Twenty-five minutes later, the seafood was done. Queen Bee turned on the television and put a DVD movie in the player.

"Y'all wanna watch *Paid In Full*?" Queen Bee asked.

"Yeah, let's watch that. I heard that's supposed to be about that dude Alpo. I wonder when they are gonna do a movie about that dude Rayful Edmonds from Washington, DC. That dude was getting paid on Orleans Place in Northeast," I said.

"I heard of him. Did you know him?" Pretty Toni asked.

"No, but I wish I had some of that money," I said.

After we ate, we finished the rest of the Grey Goose during the movie. I briefly dozed off to sleep and Pretty Toni awakened me. Queen Bee told me that they were ready for bed. I looked at Queen Bee surprisingly. I couldn't believe what she had just said. I really thought Queen Bee and I were much better than that.

I told them both that I had a nice time and walked out the door. I walked down to the end of the block to catch a cab, but the street was very dark and there was no sign of a moving vehicle in sight. Just as I stepped off the curb, a 1996 black Pathfinder pulled up and two men with guns got out and threw me in the backseat of the truck. It happened so quickly that I was in a state of shock. The two men started tying me up from my wrist to my ankles. One of them even put duct tape over my mouth. It was too late to be scared; I just prepared for death.

They took me for a long drive. All I could remember was getting on the highway and driving for about an hour. Suddenly, we stopped. I was pulled out and shot three times, once in the chest, arm, and stomach. The man that was standing behind me pulled out a straight razor and cut my throat. When I dropped to the ground, they stomped me and kicked me in my head until I was unconscious.

After they drove off leaving me for dead, I laid there bleeding like an animal that had just been slaughtered. To this day, I don't know how long I lay there, but I do know that someone saved my life.

I woke up in a hospital with five Arabian doctors

standing around my bed. When I noticed that they all wore turbans on their heads, I knew then that they were from the Middle East somewhere. They welcomed me back to the conscious world with a cup of orange juice. That was the last thing I wanted to reach for after having my throat cut open.

Somehow, I knew Pretty Toni, Gangster Joe, and Silky Slim all had something to do with what had happened to me. I kept my cool about the situation because I knew that someday I would get some get back.

About three weeks later, I was released from the hospital and needed a way to get back to Washington, DC. I called my favorite aunt, Kim, to wire me money for a bus ticket. She wired the money and I was on my way home.

On the way back to Washington, DC, I thought about Queen Bee and the girls. I even wondered if they knew what was going to happen to me before it happened. You never could tell these days because the very person you tried to extend a helping hand to would be the very one that would lay your ass down to "Rest in Peace."

With the bullet wounds in my body and the long cut across my throat, it hurt me so badly to do two things at once, like breathe and walk at the same time.

During the ride home, I met an older woman named Pat. She offered me some clothes that she had packed in a suitcase that belonged to her late husband. Pat told me that her husband had died in a car crash in St. Louis and she was here to pick up his belongings, which wasn't much. Being that the outfit I had on was severely stained with blood, grass, and mud, I accepted the change of clothes. Plus, I didn't need anything to remind me of what happened.

"What happened to you, Lucky?" Pat asked curiously.

"I was robbed, beaten, and shot several times. They also cut my throat and left me for dead," I said to her, as she slumped down in her seat.

"Did you know any of them?" Pat asked.

"In a funny sort of way, I think I do," I said, while staring out the window of the bus.

Pat had a couple of sandwiches and a few sodas in a bag, which she fed me because of my pain. At 9:46 P.M., we were pulling into the bus station on 3rd Street Northeast in Washington, DC.

"Thank God we're home!" I screamed out.

"Where do you live?" Pat asked.

"Well, I live with my aunt for now until I get my own

place," I said, as I walked off the bus.

"If you'd like, you can stay at my place tonight," Pat said with a smile on her face.

"Okay, why not? It isn't like you're Linda Blair in the movie *The Exorcist*. Or are you?" I replied with a grin.

"No, Lucky, there won't be any crazy shit like that," Pat said, laughing.

We caught a cab from the bus station to Pat's house, which was so clean you could eat off the floor.

"What a beautiful place you have, Pat," I said, while looking around the highly decorated house.

"You really like it?" Pat asked.

"Yes, it's beautiful."

Pat went upstairs to run some bath water for me to relax and to clean my wounds. My instincts told me that Pat was a good person at heart and I would need someone like her to be by my side, so I decided to make much room in my life for a woman such as her.

Months passed and I started getting better as time went by. Somehow, Pat became my number one fan, and as funny as it seemed, I became hers, as well. Pat helped me to get a job in the government, and before I knew it, a year had passed and I was on a roll.

I hadn't heard from Queen Bee and the girls until I saw Queen Bee's cousin, Tootie, at the neighborhood convenience store on 13th and D Street Northeast. Tootie told me that Queen Bee, the girls, Pretty Toni, and his two sidekicks were at her grandmother's house on 13th and Corbin Street just two blocks down the street. Instantly, I got a cold feeling of animosity and get back come over me. I asked her to describe Pretty Toni and she did to a tee.

"She's up Grandma's house right now," Tootie said.

"She?" I asked.

"Yeah, you didn't know Pretty Toni was a woman?" Tootie replied.

I laughed because I was so astonished. I could have taken a pistol and shot myself in the head; that's how much it blew my mind. Suddenly, it all came to me. How everything went in sequence, one link to another. From Queen Bee switching up on me, to the pink coloring in Pretty Toni's house, the way the bitch spelled her name, and all the shit that took place in general. All my questions were answered.

I asked Tootie if anyone else was with them, and she told me just a couple other girls from St. Louis. I gave Tootie a hug and stepped off. Death was the only thing I had on my mind.

I went over a friend's house and got his favorite weapon. He called it the beef squasher. It was an AK 47 assault rifle with an eighty-five shot clip. Each bullet was four inches long. One bullet could damage a car motor or go straight through a car from one side to the other.

After getting Pat's car, I drove to Tootie's grandmother's house. As I pulled up into a parking space, I saw three cars with St. Louis plates. I smiled and then had a flashback of what happened to me in St. Louis.

"I got you motherfuckers now!" I screamed.

I sat in the car for four hours waiting for the moment I would change their world. I watched all movement in front of the house. It seemed to me that they all smoked weed most of the day, because Blaze and Honey made several runs back and forth to the convenience store, and each time they returned, they would have blunt-type cigars.

Two more hours passed as I sat anticipating the moment I could repay Pretty Toni, Gangster Joe, and Silky Slim the bill I owed them.

Suddenly, it started raining and thundering. I saw

Tootie's grandmother's house door open, and Pretty Toni, Gangster Joe, and that flunky-ass nigga Silky Slim all ran to a 2003 red Lexus Coupe. Queen Bee and the rest of the girls ran to a separate car.

I put on a mask, got out of Pat's car, ran over to the red Lexus' driver's side window, and opened fire, hitting Pretty Toni in the head and chest eight times. Then I walked to the other side and shot Gangster Joe and Silky Slim about fourteen times each. I put some work in that night and it felt so good inside to repay them a bill that was well overdue.

I saw Queen Bee a few weeks later and she asked me if I had heard about Pretty Toni and her crew. I told her that I didn't hear a thing about it. She tried to talk to me about it, but I played it off by putting my pinky finger on her lips and saying, "Life goes on." I stepped off at that point because I didn't know if she was fishing to see if I was responsible for that shit or what.

By the time I got halfway down the block, I heard her yelling, "All the money in the world wasn't worth losing a friend like you, Lucky."

I kept on walking as though I never heard a word she said. Everything would have been cool if Queen Bee had never switched up on me to fuck with Pretty Toni, but she did and I could've lost my life due to her playing the fifty.

It wouldn't hurt me if I never saw the bitch ever again in life, because I got enough scars on my body to remember her for a lifetime.

STORY SIX
THUG ENEMY

There's an old saying that the only people that can hurt you are the people who are closest to you. At first, I never understood the science or the true meaning of that statement, until my mother gave birth to my younger brother Eric.

At the very early age of fifteen, I earned the nickname Homicide because an old redneck white man called me a black nigga boy. I pushed the redneck motherfucker down a concrete stairwell, where he busted his skull and died. I was later charged and convicted of a homicide. I pled guilty and received fifteen years under the Federal Corrections Youth Act. I spent eight years at the Lorton Youth Center-1, a youth facility center located in Lorton, Virginia.

On several occasions during my stay at Lorton, my mother would bring my little brother Eric to see me when he started to become uncontrollable. Time after time, I would talk to Eric about his bad behavior, but he would not listen; anything I had to say would go in one ear and out the other. I would find myself telling Eric stories about the terrible things that happened at Lorton. I told him how inmates would go to the canteen truck to buy goods, and how other inmates would rob them for the stuff they'd bought, and how they would take from them the packages that their families would send.

"Many inmates get raped or just plain out start fucking and sucking other inmate's dicks because they are in need of protection," I said to Eric, while my mother sat there amazed by some of the stories I told them.

I tried to scare him with the truth about jail life in hopes that he would straighten himself out, but that didn't work either. Eric had a hard fuckin' head. The boy was so damn bad that I gave him the nickname Lil' Crime.

Eight years passed and I was back on the streets again. On June 27, 1988, a very hot day of 99 degrees, I was released to a halfway house. I would always remember that day because the next day, June 28, was my birthday, and I received a social pass from my assigned counselor so I could visit my mother and brother, Lil' Crime.

I immediately caught the metro bus to my mom's place. I knocked on my mother's apartment door for about five minutes before Lil' Crime answered. As I stood knocking at the door, I started thinking and smiling to myself that I was ten years older than Lil' Crime, and it felt good to be free and still young. I was only twenty-three years old, and I still had a good chance at the life ahead of me.

"Hey, what's up, Lil' Crime?" I said, as I shook his hand.

"Is that you out there, Homicide?" my mother yelled from her dark bedroom.

"Yes, Momma, it's your oldest boy," I said, laughing.

My mother came out of her bedroom and into the living room to see me.

"Hi, baby, and happy birthday! I'm so glad you're home," Momma said, as she hugged me in her arms.

"I'm so glad to be home with my family, and this time, Momma, I plan to stay," I said, holding her tight.

"Well, baby, just remember that Momma loves you,

and if you need me, I'm always here to help you. You don't need to go in those streets for nothin'. You understand me?" Momma told me, while looking me directly in the eyes.

Momma and I walked into the kitchen, and I sat at the table. She took some barbeque short ribs, macaroni & cheese, and a mixture of kale, mustard, and turnip greens from the refrigerator. She prepared the biggest welcome home and birthday plate I had ever seen. Momma put the plate in the microwave and removed it once the timer started to beep.

When she put the plate in front of me, I looked up at her and said, "Momma, I can't eat all of this stuff!"

"Son, I want you to eat a good home cooked meal since you're back in the real world."

Just then, Lil' Crime walked into the kitchen.

"Homicide, meet my friends Terrorize and Gutta," he said, as his friends entered behind him.

"Hey, fellas, what's up?" I said, as I shook their hands.

The two kids looked to be about thirteen or fourteen. I really didn't care for the names, but what could I say? My name is Homicide and my brother's name is Lil' Crime, so what the hell. Lil' Crime, Terrorize, and Gutta seemed to go altogether.

I left Momma's place about five o'clock that evening and made my rounds throughout the neighborhood. I ran into a few guys from the old school that I had much love and respect for. The first person I saw was Action Al, a straight thug from back in the day. His criminal record consisted of murder, armed robbery, assault with intent to kill, rape while armed, bank robbery, kidnapping, and burglary. I could remember he once kidnapped a female cop, raped her, and then beheaded her. The law caught up with him, but he beat the case on a technicality. Action Al was always getting in or out of something, which is why we called him Action Al; he always had major action.

Boogie was Action Al's right-hand man. He was a bad motherfucker, too, but he was more like the driver or the lookout man when they made their moves.

I made a few moves with them in the past, but I had to control myself and not get caught up in a false image. Niggas in the street will play on you all the way around the board by using some of your defects in character to control you if you don't have any self-control. False image, which is a person being influenced and blind to a nigga's ways, and him putting you in a trick bag, is the biggest defect in a person's character.

Niggas in the street will play on that and take cold-blooded advantage of you when they see an opportunity to do so. Have you ever heard a nigga in the street say "Nigga, you getting soft"?

Some niggas might tell you to take a ride with them and never tell you that he is about to murder someone until you get there. "Here, take this pistol. I'm gonna smoke this nigga for fuckin' my girlfriend; I want you to watch my back." That's the kind of false image shit that I'm talking about, because you really don't want to be down with that type of shit for real. You just go along with that shit so you don't look like a bitch, you feel me?

I didn't hang around Action Al and Boogie for too long. We talked about the old times and drank a couple shots of Remy Martin VSOP on the corner where we stood. Soon, I was on my way continuing to make my rounds.

Later that evening when I returned to the halfway house, one of the counselors told me that I had to take a breathalyzer alcohol test because he smelled alcohol on my breath. Drinking or using illegal drugs violates halfway house rules and regulations; I was therefore sent back to jail.

Six months later, the halfway house counselors

forwarded my review and the parole board gave me a seven-year hit when I went before the board, all because of drinking alcohol.

I had to do seven years for some dumb shit. During my seven years, I found out that my little brother got locked up for armed robbery in Baltimore and spent three years in a juvenile camp. While in the camp, Lil' Crime got hooked on heroin and developed a terrible habit that led him to a life of self-destruction. I guess he felt that doing drugs would help him make it through his dark, dim, and depressing moments, but he didn't realize that his heroin habit would lead him to the ultimate roller coaster ride. When Lil' Crime was released from the Baltimore County juvenile detention camp, he returned back to my mother's place with a dope habit and a gun connection that could supply the entire United States Army.

Now that Lil' Crime was home and his childhood friends Terrorize and Gutta were at his side, the three became no holds barred in a crime infested community that surrounded them all.

"I got major motherfuckin' pull with these niggas in Baltimore; they got dope, guns, and some spots where we can chill when we rob these bitch-ass niggas," Lil Crime said, as he motioned both Terrorize and Gutta to come into our mother's apartment.

"Where is your mother"? Terrorize asked, while looking around the apartment.

"She went to the O Street Market uptown," Lil' Crime said.

"My mother went up that joint yesterday. That's a stinkin' ass place, man!" Gutta said, laughing.

"Now let's get down to business. I got six 9-millimeter handguns with three clips that hold eighteen rounds of ammunition. That's two pistols for each of us. It's time we go on some serious robberies," Lil Crime said, as he showed them the guns.

Six months had passed and Lil' Crime, Terrorize, and Gutta had robbed about 1,700 people throughout the Washington metropolitan area alone, not to mention Prince George's County and the state of Virginia. The word had spread like wildfire that Lil' Crime was my brother, and every nigga that sold drugs was out to kill him. My mother told me that some drug dealer around the area where she lived kicked her in the ass because Lil' Crime had robbed him. On several other occasions, one particular drug dealer had shot at her while driving in traffic because Lil' Crime robbed and pistol-whipped his mother until she was comatose. All over the neighborhood, Lil' Crime was known for his crude and untrustworthy reputation.

Finally, I was released from jail after serving the remaining time from my parole violation. Before I came home, I met a fine young lady during my incarceration. Her name was Star, and she stuck in there with me during my entire last bit. Star loved me and I loved her because she was real. Plus, she took real good care of me by sending me canteen money, clothing packages, letters, cards, pictures, and all of her love.

Star was a white gal from the slums of the dirty south. Star stood about 5'8" with green eyes, shoulder-length blonde hair, and an hourglass shape; every man's dream.

When I moved in with Star, I found out that she sold crack-cocaine and heroin on a very large scale. She was a powerful woman with big drugs and big money to go with it. Star gave me a job in her drug organization as a lieutenant. My job was to go around and collect money from every person she supplied. She bought me five thousand dollars worth of clothes, a motorcycle, and a 1995 BMW thirty days after I started the job.

"Homicide, I love you so much. I hope you stay with me forever," Star said, as we made love.

I had never been the type of man that could hold a woman down in a relationship for long, but I realized that I had to hold this one down because shit would have been real hard on me if it weren't for her.

Star liked to get her pussy eaten for hours. I wasn't into eating pussy, but the way she treated me, I had to learn quickly.

"Oh, shit, that's right, Homicide, eat the fuck out of my pussy. Oh, shit! Now fuck me, baby. Fuck me, please!" Star screamed, as I catered to her sexual needs.

The one good thing about me was I could fuck any bitch's pussy for five or more hours without stopping. I fucked Star for five long hours that night until her pussy was dry as the desert and as painful as a broken arm. Star said it felt like a car was speeding about one hundred miles per hour and hit her straight in that motherfucker after I finished fucking her.

"Homicide, you need to be charged with another homicide because you just killed this pussy. Goddamn!" Star said, holding her pussy with both hands.

******

My relationship with Star grew tight and stronger over the next four years, and during the fifth year, we got married. During the five years that Star and I were together, she gave birth to two beautiful kids: my son, Rasheed, who was three years old, and my now four-year-old daughter, Raysheed. Life was good for all of us as we continued to grow as a family.

One fall day, I ran into my brother Lil' Crime at my aunt's house uptown. He was down on his luck, but high as Cooter Brown. I told him that he didn't have to live like that and if he needed my help, I would be there for him. I talked it over with Star, and she had no problem with me letting Lil' Crime, Terrorize, and Gutta sell drugs for us. I brought the three of them to the house where Star, our children, and I lived.

"Damn, big brother, this is a bad-ass house," Lil' Crime said.

"Man, that's a big-ass TV in there. We can come over here and watch the Mike Tyson fights," Gutta said, as he looked around the house.

"Yeah, we'll bring the drinks. Do y'all smoke weed? We can bring that, too," Terrorize added.

"Naw, we don't smoke anything. We might take a drink

every now and again, but we don't smoke," Star replied, as she walked up the stairs.

Lil' Crime was so high from shooting heroin that he nodded and bumped his head on the dining room table.

"Ouch! Big brother, I'm sleepy as a motherfucker," Lil' Crime said, while rubbing his forehead.

"You don't have to try to fool me. I know you're high, slim. I know all the looks and the symptoms. Homicide has been around," I said.

I went downstairs to the basement to call them a cab and to get some cocaine and heroin for them to sell. I heard a lot of mumbling between the three of them, but I didn't pay any attention to it. I brought them three ounces of cocaine and one half ounce of heroin.

"Y'all owe me $3,900. That's $1,300 apiece," I said, while handing Lil' Crime the package.

"We can handle that, big bro. Give us about a week and we'll be right back at you, slim," Lil Crime said loudly.

"Man, lower your voice. I don't want the neighbors to hear you, slim," I said.

"You right; my fault," Lil' Crime responded.

Fifteen minutes later, a cab was in front of my house

blowing the horn for them. I walked them out front, we shook hands, and they got into the cab. After watching them pull away in the cab, I walked back into the house and chilled with my wife and children.

The next morning, Star told me that she was cool with me giving Lil' Crime a helping hand, but she didn't like the idea of them coming to our house.

"Homicide, you never bring a nigga to the place where you lay your head," Star said, as she began to cook breakfast.

"You're right, but that's my brother. He'll never cross me," I said.

Star gave me a strange look. "Niggas would cross God if they got the chance," Star mumbled, as she kissed both of the kids.

A week later, Lil' Crime, Terrorize, and Gutta were sitting on my front steps when Star, the kids, and I pulled up in front of the house.

"See what the fuck I'm talking about! Look at this shit, man," Star said, as she pointed at them.

Lil' Crime could tell that Star didn't like the fact that they were sitting on our steps, not to mention being at our home when we weren't there.

"I'm sorry if it's a problem. We didn't know if y'all was home or not, so we just took the chance to see. We didn't mean any harm," Lil' Crime said, as they followed us into the house.

"That doesn't sit well with me, Lil' Crime. I don't want my neighbors in my business. That's what I'm saying! I don't see why he brought y'all out here in the first place. Homicide, you should know better!" Star yelled.

I looked at Lil' Crime, Terrorize, and Gutta, and it seemed as if they had some animosity about Star yelling out at them the way she did, but they held their composure like true diplomats. The silence between them caught my attention, but I didn't think much of it.

Lil' Crime paid me every dime the three of them owed. I gave the money to Star, and then I went to the safe in the basement and brought them 125 grams of powder cocaine and two ounces of heroin.

"Damn, Homicide, I'm glad you fuck with us like this. You and Star really look out for us. Thanks, big brother," Lil' Crime said, as I put the drugs in a backpack for them.

As usual, Lil' Crime and his partners called a cab and went on their way.

I went upstairs to chill with Star and the kids, but when I looked in the kids' room, they were asleep.

"I want to have crazy sex with my husband!" Star said when I walked into our bedroom.

"That's a great idea. Let's fuck!" I responded.

Star looked at me with those pretty green eyes. "Do you have to say it like that? Let's fuck! Can you be a bit more romantic?" Star asked, as I began to give her oral sex. "Oh, my goodness. Oh, my goodness!" Star kept screaming repeatedly, as I gave her my vicious head. "I love you, Homicide! I love you! Oh, baby, I love you so much!"

Thirty minutes later, I started fuckin' the dog shit out of her.

"I love you, too, baby," I said, while banging that pussy from the back.

Another thirty minutes had passed, and I was fast asleep, lying on top of Star in her arms.

At about 3 A.M., Star and I were awakened to the sound of a loud outburst of noise; the front door had been knocked off its hinges. I jumped out of bed and ran to the top of the stairs. I saw three men with guns in their hands and masks over their heads running up the stairs headed toward our bedroom. I quickly went back into the bedroom and held onto my wife. The three men burst into our bedroom and shot my wife straight in the head at pointblank range. She died instantly with her eyes wide open. One of the men went into my kids' bedroom, tied my son up, and blindfolded him.

"Where is the other kid, motherfucker?" the gunman screamed at me.

"She's at her grandmother's house," I said.

I didn't know where my daughter was at that point because I had just checked on her and my son a few hours earlier, but I kinda figured she was safe.

The gunmen made me open the safe in the basement and give them all of the dope and money, which totaled fifteen kilos of cocaine, ten kilos of heroin, and $975,000 in cash.

It was strange and crazy, but deep down inside I knew it would someday come to this. Everybody's story was the same; something or someone would stop a nigga from getting their grind on.

The three gunmen made me and my son get in my bedroom closet. They then tied me up and put duct tape around my wrists and legs. After closing the door, they shot through the door twelve times before leaving. I was hit all twelve times in the chin, stomach, arm, leg, and foot, but somehow survived my injuries. My son was not hit at all, thank God. I found out later that my daughter had hidden in a hole in the ceiling of her closet.

Seven days later, Star's parents and I held her wake and funeral. Seven days after that, my daughter testified to a grand jury that she saw my brother, Terrorize, and Gutta pull the masks from off their faces as they left our house.

That was fucked up. I never thought in a million years that my brother would be my enemy. That nigga put on a great show at Star's funeral, cryin' and all that shit, but the truth came out and he would pay for it.

The only thing I couldn't understand was the motive. Star and I had extended our hand to all of them and they didn't have to do that shit.

Star was right; you never bring a motherfucker to your home. Always watch the person that's closest to you because jealousy is a motherfucker.